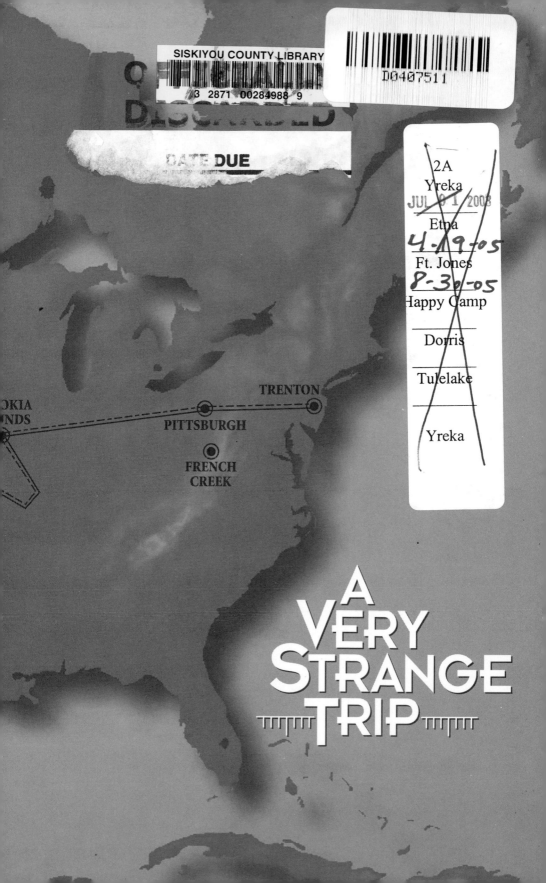

TRENTON

OKIA
NDS

PITTSBURGH

FRENCH
CREEK

A VERY STRANGE TRIP

A VERY STRANGE TRIP

Other Selected Works by the Authors

L. RON HUBBARD

DAVE WOLVERTON

AN ORIGINAL STORY BY

L. RON HUBBARD

NOVEL BY

DAVE WOLVERTON

A VERY STRANGE TRIP

Bridge Publications, Inc.

A VERY STRANGE TRIP
© 1999 L. Ron Hubbard Library
All rights reserved

For information, address Bridge Publications, Inc.,
4751 Fountain Ave., Los Angeles, CA 90029

Front cover photograph entitled Pyramids of the Moon
and Sun, Teotihuacan courtesy of ALTI Publishing.

ISBN 1-57318-164-1

10 9 8 7 6 5 4 3 2 1

Preface

A little over fifteen years ago, L. Ron Hubbard published a science-fiction novel, *Battlefield Earth,* which became one of the bestselling and best-loved novels in its field. (That work has since sold over five million copies and a recent Random House Modern Library readers' poll ranked it among the top three best novels of the twentieth century.)

At the same time, as Ron reentered the field of science fiction after a hiatus of nearly thirty years, he recognized how closed the genre had become to new authors. I happened to be a new author fifteen years ago, and I well recall studying the markets for short fiction only to find that among the top four science-fiction magazines, perhaps no more than ten new writers might be published in any given year.

As on other occasions throughout his 55-year literary career, Ron came up with a great idea to help aspiring writers enter the professional ranks. He initiated a contest to encourage new writers and call attention to their work. He even arranged for top writers of speculative fiction (science fiction, fantasy and horror) to judge the competition.

Thus L. Ron Hubbard's WRITERS OF THE FUTURE® Contest was born. It has since discovered and helped launch the careers of hundreds of talented writers who have gone on to publish over 250 novels and over 2,000 short stories. It is widely recognized as the premier venue in the field for discovering new writing talent. The L. Ron Hubbard Gold Award, which goes to the annual grand-prize winner, has taken its place beside the Hugo and Nebula Awards as one of the most coveted prizes in the field of speculative fiction. There is even a companion contest for new illustrators.

My own involvement in the Contest began with a recommendation from M. Shayne Bell, who had previously received a first-place quarterly prize. Shortly thereafter, I, too, managed a first-place award, then a grand prize in 1987. I will never forget the annual awards ceremony, being sandwiched between the likes of Isaac Asimov, Frederik Pohl and Luke Skywalker himself, Mark Hamil. But more to the point, and just as Ron intended, that award most definitely helped launch my writing career. Indeed, I received a three-novel contract from Bantam Books barely two weeks later.

Needless to say, that award brought something else; for as Ron also suggested to his literary agency, Author Services, Inc., some of those newly discovered writers were to be afforded what amounted to a collaboration with Ron. In other words, some of us were to be given a golden opportunity to place our names on a story by L. Ron Hubbard. Of course, I myself was among those so honored, and found it to be a fulfilling collaboration.

The story Ron originally conceived, *A Very Strange Trip,* became a full-length L. Ron Hubbard screenplay, replete with detailed directorial notes, character sketches and more. What I initially found most intriguing, however, was the fact that the story concerned the time-traveling adventures of a young West Virginian moonshiner, who inadvertently finds himself purchasing Native American squaws.

It just so happens my grandfather was also a moonshiner from West Virginia, and likewise purchased a half-Cherokee wife, my grandmother. It was all strictly illegal, but grandpa never worried too much about legalities. Moreover, it was all part and parcel of my grandmother's cultural heritage, as her mother had similarly been sold to her father and so on . . . from time immemorial.

To some degree, then, writing this book gave me an opportunity to rediscover my personal heritage. Then, too, I had long dreamed of studying paleobiology, and here was an opportunity to delve rather deeply into the realms of mammoths and dinosaurs. Finally, I had wanted to try my hand at writing comedy, a rare element in science fiction.

But there was another aspect to L. Ron Hubbard's *A Very Strange Trip* that immediately intrigued me, and therein lies something of the L. Ron Hubbard legend.

In the name of research, I eventually traveled to the Cahokia Mounds where the Mississippi and Missouri Rivers meet—once home to the temples of the priest-rulers of the Mississippian culture. And what did I inevitably discover? In one sense or another, Ron, too, had made that trek and, I might add, researched these matters to the bone. In point of fact, I found no aspect of ancient life in these lands that Ron did not examine—from a study of Mississippian vegetation to the Mayan pottery industry.

Yet remembering that a screenplay is not a book, and the art of adapting a tale from one medium to another often requires some innovation, let me add one final word of introduction. Because scripted comedy does not always play on paper, I could not always translate, so to speak, Ron's story word for word. By the same token, however, a novel allows one to read a character's thoughts, and so I afforded myself a degree of literary latitude in just that sense—interpreting the thoughts of Ron's characters.

I hope the result is as fun for you to read as it was for Ron and me to write.

Dave Wolverton

CHAPTER 1

"The prisoner will now rise for sentencing," the bailiff of the Upshaw County Superior Court intoned with a solemn expression, stopping in mid-chaw to hold a wad of tobacco in the side of his mouth.

Nineteen-year-old Everett Dumphee stood and smoothed back a lick of his blond hair. He was big and strong-boned. He quietly made sure his flannel shirt was tucked into his new pair of Wrangler jeans, and stared at the judge with a heart brimful of dread.

Beside Dumphee, his girl, Jo Beth, sat quietly and held his hand. Everett's ma and pappy, and uncles and cousins were all packed into the courthouse. The benches could not have held more of them. Even the old preacher who lived in the cave up by Blue Grouse Creek had come down for the court appearance.

Judge Wright was middle aged, slightly chubby, and he was staring hard at Everett with a mean look in his eye, like a hound that's holed himself a 'coon. Judge Wright glared a minute, then said, "Everett Dumphee, you've been found guilty of runnin' moonshine. Before I sentence you, do you have anything to say for yourself?"

Dumphee cleared his throat, found it hard to talk. "Uh, I didn't do it, Your Honor, sir."

Judge Wright made a little snarling face, as if Dumphee had poked him in the belly with a sharp stick. "I don't want to hear *that!* I know it was your uncle's car, and you said you was late for a date. But you was caught red-handed, drivin' down old Bald Knob at ninety miles an hour with ten gallons of shine in your trunk—and when the police flashed their lights, you revved it up to a hundred and forty!"

Dumphee's pappy shouted, "Aw, he's just born with good reflexes, Your Honor! You can't blame the boy for that."

"You shut your yap in my courthouse," Judge Wright said, pointing the gavel at Dumphee's pappy. "If your boy has such good driving instincts, put him on the racing circuit—not runnin' shine!" The judge cleared his throat, tried to regain his composure.

"Now, Everett Dumphee, I'm a fair man—or at least I try to be . . ." the judge said sweetly. "But I'm tired as get-out of you Dumphees running shine. My grandpappy sent your grandpappy to prison for it. My pappy sent your pappy to prison for it. And I'd send you to prison right now, but for one thing: you Dumphees can't help it that you're all so inbred that you ain't bright enough to figure out right from wrong."

Dumphee's mother gasped, and Dumphee spoke up, trying to defend the family honor, "Uh, sir, I ain't—"

"You've had plenty of chance to say your piece!" the judge brushed him off. "Now I'm going to say my piece. Dumphee, boy, your problem is that you're *uncivilized*. You give West Virginia a bad name. You live up in them hollows with your dogs and your guns and your moonshine, marrying your cousins and playing your fiddles. Jethro Clampett has got nothing on you—"

"Uh, Bodine," Dumphee said.

"What?" Judge Wright asked.

"Jethro *Bodine* is his name. Jed Clampett is his uncle. I watched that show on TV, and Bodine is his name. We get 140 channels on our satellite dish, now."

"Are you trying to be a wiseacre with me?" the judge asked.

"Uh, no, sir," Dumphee said, affecting a thick accent. Judge Wright always talked with a thick accent, as if he thought that he sounded like some southern gentleman. But the truth was, with modern television pumping educated standard American English into every home in the hills, practically no one in West Virginia spoke like the judge did anymore. Dumphee thought the judge sounded like a hick. Still, it sometimes helped to sound like one of the good ol' boys.

The judge said, "Because I've got a hundred *acres* of good farmland at home, I don't need no *wise*acre, and if you are being a wiseacre with me . . ."

3

"No, suh!" Dumphee said louder, in an even thicker accent.

"My point is, this is 1991. Everyone else up in those hills is trying to raise marijuana and driving Porsches. But you folks— you're living in the past." The judge shook his head so woefully, Dumphee almost wished that he were a marijuana farmer, just so he'd get some respect. At Dumphee's side, his pappy was stiffening, getting red in the face, blood pressure rising so high, Dumphee feared he might burst a vessel.

The judge sighed. "You got to go out and see the world, son. So, I'm going to do you a favor. I'm going to civilize you."

The judge took a long, deep breath, stared Dumphee in the face. "I hereby sentence you to the maximum penalty for your crime: ten years of watching television in the West Virginia State Prison."

The words hit Dumphee like a fist in the belly. It was so unfair. He really hadn't been running shine. He hadn't known that his uncle had that keg in the back! It wasn't fair that he'd go to prison. Didn't the judge know what men did to each other in there?

At his side, Jo Beth squeezed Dumphee's hand and whined. "I'll wait for you," she promised, while his ma broke down sobbing. His pappy's face was so red that Dumphee figured the old man would go out to the truck, get his rifle, and find a shady tree to lay under while he waited for the judge to poke his head out of the courthouse.

But now the judge was shaking his head sadly.

"That's right, son. I said 'prison.' But if that don't sit well with you, then I'll set aside that penalty on one condition: you enlist in the United States Army for a period of no less than five years—I do suppose you can shoot?"

"He can knock the eye out of a red-tailed hawk at three hundred yards, Your Honor!" Dumphee's cousin shouted.

"Yeah, I ought to fine him $500 right now for shooting raptors," the judge grumbled. "Well, I figured as much. And you look strong enough to wrestle a bear. What do you say? You can avoid prison, and this will give you a chance to get out of them hills, see the world.

"Some folks say you can take a boy out of the mountains, but you can't take the mountains out of the boy. I don't know if I believe 'em. You'll either come back a new and better man, or else you'll be the Rambo of moonshiners."

Dumphee stood, seething. It wasn't fair. He had plans for his life. Plans for him and Jo Beth!

He wasn't a hillbilly. It was true that his family engaged in moonshining, but this wasn't unsophisticated hooch stewed up in a bathtub. His pa had a computer, and got orders over the Internet. Some English fellow would send e-mail, telling what he wanted, then send bottles to fill with names like "Boar's Breath" and "Hair of the Hound o' Morgan"—sophisticated whiskeys out of Scotland and Ireland.

Sure, the Dumphees were selling forgeries—and had been making a lot of money at it for the past twenty years—but in the past few months the whole family business had begun to go somewhat legitimate. The new "Dumphee Clan" whiskeys were selling better in France than the forged labels ever had.

What did this hoary old judge know about civilization? He probably thought that the Internet was some fancy new device used to catch a trout!

And as for his Porsches, well, the old souped-up T-bird that the government had confiscated could outrun one of them overpriced, unreliable Porsches any day!

The judge stared at Dumphee expectantly. He offered, "What do you say, son? The Army, or prison?

"The Army would be easy for a fellow like you, what with the Soviet Union falling apart. I wish we had a war I could send you into, but I figure, given five years of enlistment, something ought to come along. . . ."

And if you're lucky, I'll get shot, Dumphee thought. He sighed.

"Guess I'll have to take the Army, Your Honor," Dumphee said, feeling queasy.

Jo Beth squeezed his hand. He figured he could always send for her after he got out of basic training. They could get themselves on the waiting list for some little dumpy army apartment.

Hell, Dumphee thought with resignation, at least he isn't making me enlist in the Navy.

"Bailiff, remand this boy to the custody of the U.S. Army," the judge said.

Everyone stood up a bit dumbfounded. Everett's uncle came and slapped Dumphee's shoulder, apologized for getting him in trouble.

Jo Beth fell apart and started weeping. "Oh, Everett," she said, trembling as she leaned against his shoulder. "This is so terrible. So terrible."

"It won't be that bad," Dumphee said.

She sniffed. "You're always so positive. 'If life hands you a lemon, make lemonade.' That's the way I've got to think. I just—I just always knew you would make it out of these mountains someday, but I never thought it would be like this. I thought you'd go to college."

"Well, I still can go to college," Dumphee said. "Just looks like I'll be doing it on the GI Bill." He'd always been good in school. Not brilliant, but he imagined himself to be a cut above average. Given that, and the fact that Dumphee was a fighter, he'd always figured he'd do okay in college.

Dumphee's wrists were cuffed, so he couldn't hug Jo Beth, but she just squeezed his hands and leaned into him. He could smell the sweet perfume on her neck, feel her pleasant curves through the fabric of her cotton dress. "I'll join you, after you get out of basic training. I'd wait for you, even if it took till the end of time. Nothing can keep us apart."

The bailiff took Dumphee right then and led him down to the recruiter's office in handcuffs. He got to stop once, outside the courthouse, to say goodbye to the redbone hunting hounds in the back of his pappy's pickup.

Then he was gone.

CHAPTER 2

Dumphee had seen the Army propaganda on TV: "Be all that you can be," the advertisements said.

But, apparently, the Army figured that Dumphee wasn't fit for much. Some sergeant took one look at his record, and chewed his lip thoughtfully for all of half a second. "Moonshine running? At 140 mph? Boy'd make a hell of a driver!"

So they sent him to basic training down in Georgia.

Yet part of Dumphee recognized that his life was being stolen from him, bit by bit, minute by minute. The recognition first hit when Jo Beth wrote him a letter a week into basic training, telling how his cousin, Montague Dumphee, was being such a sweetheart and comforting her through this lonely transition period.

Dumphee had always known that Montague wanted his girl. Last fall, when they'd been out on the big annual family bear hunt with Uncle Ned, Montague had asked Dumphee all kinds of disturbing questions about "how far he'd got" with Jo Beth. And he'd had an unsavory gleam in his eye. Dumphee fired off a letter forbidding Jo Beth to have anything to do with the boy.

But by the time the U.S. Mail got the letter to her, it was probably already too late. She wrote back and told Dumphee how Montague had taken her on "a couple of picnics," and how he was a real gentleman, and she didn't like Dumphee slandering "my Montague."

Two weeks later, Dumphee got a call from his ma. Jo Beth and Montague had moved into a little house outside Bald Knob.

It all happened so fast, Dumphee felt stung. Something important had been taken from him—twenty-four days of his life. And in that meager time, the woman he'd planned to marry, the woman who'd promised to wait for him through ten years of prison, had run off with his cousin.

It's amazing how love for a woman can make a smart man act stupid. Dumphee walked around like a wounded critter for half a week, and during a live-grenade practice, for all of two seconds he held on to a live one, wondering how Jo Beth would feel if he just tucked that grenade down his undershirt and let it blow his heart to bits.

Then he figured, Naw, she ain't worth it, and he imagined Montague's leering face and chucked the grenade toward it, setting a new camp distance record for hurling a grenade.

For the rest of basic training, the boys in his platoon called him "The Launcher."

But the appellation didn't stick.

Dumphee didn't really mind basic training, and it appeared that being a driver wouldn't be so bad after all. It beat being on the front lines if he went to war. He was transferred to a driving school in Virginia, where he learned the basics, like how to change a wiper blade and tighten a fan belt.

After that, he concentrated on advanced army driving techniques, like how to "dodge-and-drive" in case someone began shooting out your windshield while you tried to deliver some general to an Arab liquor store.

And he soon learned to spot mines hidden under the road like a pro. None of the driving instructors in the school had ever seen anyone with "instincts" like his. Dumphee figured it came from having to watch out for chuckholes on West Virginia highways. Whatever the reason for his unexpected skill, he soon learned to enjoy showing off his abilities by driving through a live minefield at eighty miles an hour.

※

On his first assignment, he was supposed to report to a major whose motto was "Any soldier who isn't in combat isn't in uniform unless he's in *dress* uniform."

Dumphee was becoming adept at dealing with quack officers, so he was in full dress, in the driving rain, when he passed a sign beside the road. The rain was pouring so hard that even at thirty-five miles per hour, even with his high beams pointed up and adjusted to the right (he'd gone out in the rain with his screwdriver and turned one headlight so that it shone upward), he still couldn't read the sign. The pounding of the windshield wipers vied for loudness with the beating of rain on the hood of the truck.

"Lieutenant? Lieutenant Fugg?" Dumphee said. Fugg lay asleep, his head resting on the glass of the passenger door. Dumphee pushed him slightly. "Sir, wake up! I think we've lost the convoy. What do we do?"

The lieutenant, a stocky little fellow with bug-eyed glasses, roused a bit and grumbled, "Trenton Arsenal Experimental Weaponry."

"Yessir, yessir, I know where we're headed," Dumphee said. "But how do I get there?"

"Hell, Private," Fugg said as if he were a general, "you're supposed to be the best moonshine driver in West Virginia. Just drive."

"Yessir," Dumphee said, "but this ain't West Virginia. I think we're in Pennsylvania. Or maybe New Jersey—"

"Shut up!" Lieutenant Fugg said, annoyed. He nuzzled up to the fogged glass of his window.

A truck whizzed past in the opposite direction, and just afterward, Dumphee saw a sign, *Levittown, Pennsylvania.*

"Just keep on this road," Fugg said, as he closed his eyes to sleep.

Well, Dumphee thought, as pappy always used to say, "If I got to be lost, at least I can be lost *faster* than anyone else, and maybe I'll find myself quicker in the bargain." With that, Dumphee shifted the truck into a higher gear.

Dumphee felt out of sorts. He hadn't gotten much sleep since basic training, and here he was on his first driving assignment, and his lieutenant wasn't going to be any help at all. He wished he could stop somewhere and ask directions, or look at a map or something. But he was in a hurry, and this truck sure couldn't hit 140, so he kept driving, the sweat breaking out on him as he passed sign after sign: *Fallsington, Pennsylvania; White Horse* (no state listed); *Yardville, New Jersey.* Heck, he was driving through half the country and all the time his gas tank was draining lower and lower, and he never saw sign of another army truck. Fugg kept snoring. *Robbinsville. Windsor, New Jersey.*

Then there it was: Trenton Arsenal. Dumphee whistled in relief as the truck coasted into the compound, the gas gauge well below empty. Just as he began to apply the brakes, the engine sputtered and died.

Through the falling rain, Dumphee could see a large truck back into the loading bay of a warehouse. It was a strange truck—typical army olive in color, covered with canvas on top—but the wheels were huge, thickly treaded and shaped like giant balloons. The bottom of the truck looked like a boat, with a rudder on back. Dumphee had seen plenty of hunters with ATVs up in the hills, but nothing this size.

There in the rain, pacing back and forth in front of the truck, was a major strutting around like a Patton wannabe. The major looked on impatiently as the vehicle was loaded, a cigar clenched between his teeth, and slapped at his boots with a swagger stick. Dumphee had never seen a swagger stick outside of the movies, and he wondered where the major had purchased it. Was it government issue?

Dumphee was dressed to the teeth. He didn't want to get his uniform wet. He rolled down the window.

The major glanced at him, demanding, "Where the hell is the rest of your convoy, Private?"

Dumphee climbed down from the cab of his truck, stood looking at the major, and saluted. He held that salute a long time, letting it shield his eyes from the rain. He'd hoped that the other trucks would be here by now. Dumphee read the fellow's nametag: *Slice. Major Slice.* Dumphee didn't know quite what to say. Weeks of basic training had left him so messed up in the head that he felt more terrified of his commanding officers than of enemy gunfire—which of course was the main reason for basic training in the first place. He swallowed hard and said, "I don't know where the rest of the convoy is, Major, sir. We got lost in the rain."

Slice grumbled under his breath, almost a growl. "Where is your commanding officer? Who is in charge here?"

Dumphee almost said, "I thought you were in charge," but he realized it might sound mouthy. "Lieutenant Fugg is in charge of the convoy, sir. He's asleep in the truck."

"Asleep, is he?" Slice asked.

Slice turned and marched through the rain with a disgruntled air. Dumphee was afraid of what would happen next, so he rushed to the other side of his truck, following the major.

Slice went to the door. Fugg's sleeping face was plastered against the window, looking like some rubber mask.

Slice jerked the door open.

The lieutenant took a clumsy fall from the truck and landed on his head.

Slice stood for a moment, as if mesmerized, trying to recount in his head exactly how Fugg had spun during the fall. He twirled his finger in a downward spiral, made a tiny splat sound. Then he said heavily, "Lieutenant Fugg, with moves like that, you could someday make a fine addition to the United States Olympic dive team. But I am not at *all* sure what kind of soldier you might be."

"What? What?" Fugg said, looking up groggily.

"Sleeping on duty is akin to treason, boy," Slice said. "I'd shoot you between the eyes right now, but I'm afraid the recruiters would only send me worse. Now, get in my office!"

CHAPTER 3

In the shipping office, boxes, papers and packages sat all along the walls from floor to ceiling. Many boxes were marked with Cyrillic characters and featured official stamps with the red sickle and hammer—Russian customs stamps.

In the middle of the floor was one such box, about five feet in length, two in width and three feet high. On top of all the Russian notations, yellow tape with black characters shouted *Top-Secret* from almost every corner of the package.

Major Slice took a seat behind a table, purposely blanked a screen on the office computer, and then held Fugg's eye. Dumphee had helped the lieutenant to a chair by the desk. Fugg's fall had left him somewhat groggy.

Pointedly ignoring Fugg's current state of incapacitation, Slice said, "Now listen up, Fugg. This is a very important mission!" He swatted the desk with his swagger stick for emphasis.

Lieutenant Fugg's head nodded to the desk. Dumphee nudged him. Fugg lifted his chin, studied the major from half-closed eyes.

Slice gazed at Fugg menacingly. "Soldier, have you been drinking on duty or something?"

The lieutenant didn't answer. "No, sir," Dumphee said. "I think it was the fall. He hurt his head."

Major Slice chewed thoughtfully on his cigar a moment. "Nonsense," he grumbled. "He's an American soldier. A good soldier is born with a bulletproof head."

Slice went back into his lecturing tone. "Our whole battalion in Denver is waiting for this box. And this box must get to Denver without a jolt! 'Cause if you jolt, jar, bump, tip, bounce—or otherwise disturb—this crate, there will be hell to pay."

Dumphee, startled by this news, glanced at the box. He wondered what was in it. Some kind of experimental explosive?

"This package is far too sensitive to go by air or rail," the major said. Then he beamed a smile. "So we've provided you with a new transport vehicle. It's one of a kind, designed to give the softest ride available. And with an expert driver—"

"See, you got it wrong, too," Dumphee said. "Just like the judge. I'm really not a moonshine driver. Now my uncle Claude—"

"What is your name, soldier?" the major shouted, not bothering to squint to read Dumphee's nametag.

"Dumphee. Private Dumphee, sir."

"And your Military Occupational Specialty?"

Dumphee faltered. "I guess I'm a driver. . . . But I was kind of hoping they'd send me to school to be a computer programmer—"

"You *guess* you're a driver? You don't have to *guess* about it, son. You *are* a driver!" the major growled. His tone said that he didn't want any arguments. "You have been trained by the finest military machine in the world, and if you weren't one hell of a driver, you wouldn't be sent on this mission."

"Yessir," Dumphee said thoughtfully, unconvinced. He didn't really want to haul dangerous cargo. He said weakly, "Is there some kind of a backpack nuke in that box?"

Fugg's head had nodded back down to the table. Dumphee sort of reached over and pulled the lieutenant's head upright.

Major Slice looked left and right as if to make certain that they were alone in the room. He leaned forward conspiratorially and whispered, "All right, son, listen up. This is all Top-Secret, but you've got a right to know." Slice nodded toward the box in the center of the room and said, "As you may realize, with the fall of the Soviet Union, just about everything is up for sale—MIGs, nuclear submarines, their entire space program. What we've got in these packages all came straight from the Russian Army's research and development teams. This is all very, very secret. Hell, the prime minister of Russia himself probably doesn't know what half this stuff is.

"So, we've bought all this equipment, and now we need to get it to Denver where it can be tested. But there's a problem. . . ."

At this, Slice bent forward and whispered. "See, we bought this advanced equipment, but we sort of got it from some middlemen. Understand? It seems that some old Russian generals don't want it to fall into our hands. I have to be honest, gentlemen. Russian agents could be anywhere on the road between here and Denver."

Dumphee nodded.

Slice continued, "They won't hesitate to kill you for the contents of that box."

Dumphee stared at the box, horror sinking into his chest.

"So I'm counting on you—Dumphee, Fugg."

The lieutenant made a sound like "Glug."

Dumphee's heart pounded. He said, "Uh, Major, uh, sir— what does the box do?"

Slice glanced at his watch. "Oh, it's sort of a machine that distorts time or something. We've got some pinhead mathematicians in Denver who can explain it to you better than I could. You know, you can buy just about anything in Russia nowadays—and I *mean* anything! If you boys were smart, you'd invest in the Russian mail-order bride business right now! Are you boys married?"

Dumphee shook his head no.

"For about $2,000 they could line you up with a Moscow model so gorgeous, you'd think that Christie Brinkley was her ugly kid sister. I mean *everything's* for sale. You wouldn't believe it.

"Well, I've got to go pick up my wife and kids so I can catch a plane to Denver." Slice stood, slapped his boot with the swagger stick, and headed toward the door.

The major seemed to have another thought. "Oh, and gentlemen," he said with a scowl, "if you make it to Denver one minute late, there will be court-martials waiting for you." His voice took a lower, more ominous tone. "Good luck."

The major had hardly left the room when Master Sergeant Allred entered the room, a stack of manifest papers in hand. "Oh, there you are. All ready to get this time machine gizmo off our hands, I see."

Allred turned, yelled through a door. "Off your butts, guys. Truck to load!"

Dumphee asked, "Is that thing really dangerous? The major said—"

Allred grunted, "Officers schmofficers. Ain't you got a sergeant or somebody reliable with you?" He glanced out the back door, then turned back to Dumphee. "You only got one truck?"

Dumphee tried to get Fugg to sit up straight, but the lieutenant kept slumping forward. Dumphee said, "Uh, ah—there were two more, but I guess they took a wrong turn."

Allred shook his papers in Dumphee's face. "Well, hell! Do you think we're just a dumping ground for your whole god-damned battalion? We've got experimental assault rifles, bazookas, fifty thousand rounds of ammunition, grenades!" Allred stared at his papers. "We've got to get them shipped somehow! Looks like you're going to have to carry the whole load."

21

A couple of privates shifted the time machine onto a dolly. A sign that had been on the bottom of the box now showed: *DO NOT JOLT!*

Allred shouted at the privates: "You men, get all the rest of that junk on this truck, too."

The privates began to hustle. Lieutenant Fugg got up and shook his head slowly, as if to clear it. "Dumphee, you take over here for a moment, I'm going to find me a coffee machine."

The faint aroma of coffee wafted from the secretary's room outside the major's office. As Fugg headed in to help himself to some of the major's brew, Dumphee watched the fellows load the box with rising concern.

"Sergeant," Dumphee said to Allred. "That box we're hauling is marked *Do Not Jolt*, but your men are just going to throw it on the vehicle!"

"Oh, they'll be careful," the sergeant barked, loud enough to warn his loaders.

The privates carefully set the crate in the middle of the ATV, came back in for some of the Russian experimental rifles, and one of them smiled wickedly at Dumphee as he tossed the bundle of rifles atop the box.

Dumphee's heart pounded. If anything got damaged, he'd take the blame.

"Sergeant," he appealed to Allred, "I don't think they ought to do that!"

The sergeant made brutal slashing marks with his pen as each package was thrown atop the others, then glared at

Dumphee. "That's the load!" he called, when the last package landed in the ATV.

Dumphee said, "But, I don't think we should have all that stuff on top of the box!"

Allred glared at Dumphee. "I said, 'That's the load.'"

"Right," Dumphee said. "Yessir, that's the load."

CHAPTER 4

By the time Dumphee got Fugg into the ATV, the lieutenant was looking much better. At least he could hold his head up without nodding so much. But when Lieutenant Fugg took off his hat, there was a huge knot on his head.

Dumphee glanced down at the controls for the ATV. The keys were already in it. He turned the key and hit the gas. The control panels lighted up like something from a spaceship—showing longitude, latitude, elevation, compasses. A little holographic display flashed up on the windshield, showing a map of area roads, all in blue. Another display beside it was marked *Infrared View*. Though rain poured down so hard outside that Dumphee could hardly see fifty feet, the infrared display showed fine detail that the naked eye just couldn't detect.

Dumphee fumbled through the glove compartment, searching for a manual for the vehicle, but didn't find one.

The steering wheel was like the joystick on a plane. By pulling it back, the front of the vehicle raised just a bit—it used hydraulics to help keep the load in back level while going up- or downhill. A red button to his left was marked *Armaments*. Dumphee pushed the button.

A fifty-millimeter gun swiveled up from a concealed port above the right wheel well, and a small display showed that the vehicle also held two pairs of missiles in launch tubes beneath the chassis. A lighted control panel displayed the options for arming and firing the missiles and guns.

"You're in trouble now, Darth Vader," Dumphee whispered. He imagined the damage he could do if some fool cut him off in traffic, and sort of wished he had something like this at home.

"Well, Lieutenant, where do we go?"

"Denver," Fugg said.

"Yeah, but how do we get there?" Dumphee asked. Then he noticed something odd. As soon as Fugg had said "Denver," a little trail was marked out in red flashing dots on the map that glowed on his windshield. The red dots looked like animated red corpuscles flowing through a vein.

This vehicle had a computer with voice recognition, Dumphee realized. He'd been reading computer magazines at school, and knew at least that much about them. "New York," he said. The lines on the map changed.

"Not New York!" Fugg said, holding his head. "Denver."

The lines on the map changed again, and Dumphee gently put his foot on the gas. His ATV suddenly showed up as a yolk-colored blip moving among the red dots.

"Good going, Artoo," Dumphee said. "Now see if you can lock down those rear stabilizers."

Fugg looked at the map on the windshield. "Ah, geez, my head hurts. Listen, you're the driver. You got the map. So just—you and Yoda can get us there. Use the Force, Dumphee."

Dumphee tried to take it very easy, accelerating slowly so as not to jar his precious cargo. The engine was so quiet, Dumphee could hardly feel it, and as the ATV began rolling through the compound, it seemed to float like a cloud over the road. The vehicle had an automatic transmission that shifted so smoothly, you could never feel it pop into a new gear.

Outside, the rain pelted down in sheets, and suddenly a burst of lightning flashed through the clouds, snarling. The truck drove so quietly that as Dumphee pulled out onto the highway the only sounds were the beating of the windshield wipers, the pounding of rain on the cab, and Fugg's gentle snoring.

Dumphee drove long into the night, and the sound of the wipers thudded in time with the blood pounding through his veins, making a tune. In his mind, he put the tune to the fiddle and guitar, banjo and washboard and silently began to sing.

Windshield wipers pounding in the rain.
Wish I could see my sweetheart again.

It's getting late and the lights are low.
Driving in the darkness. Go, car, go.

He hadn't heard Jo Beth's voice in weeks, and he wondered if he could go find her. He longed to head back to the mountains. Aloud, he said the words "Bald Knob, West Virginia," and watched the map on the dashboard change colors.

The sight only made his heart ache.

Beside him, Lieutenant Fugg snored softly and grunted, "Anchovies and onions on that burger, sweetheart." Then he smiled pleasantly in his sleep.

Dumphee followed road signs toward Pennsylvania, heading for Pittsburgh and environs beyond. Somewhere in the night, he saw a sign: *You are now changing time zones. Set your clock back one hour.*

Everything was going fine until a siren shrieked in the cab and lights on the dashboard began flashing in shades of blue, green and red.

"Incoming!" Fugg screamed, flailing his arms, rising from his sleep. His eyes went wide. "We're on fire or something! This truck is on fire! What the hell is going on?"

Dumphee studied the dashboard. A mechanical voice announced, "Warning! Warning! You are low on gas. You are low on gas."

Dumphee said, "I, uh, think we're low on gas."

"Gas? Gas? All this noise for gas? Damn!" Fugg said, holding his heart, eyes wide. "I thought it must be a nuclear war."

The map flashed the route to the nearest gas station. Dumphee pulled off at a turnpike and headed into a small town, to an all-night gas station.

He pulled up to the pumps, got out and walked around the vehicle several times, looking for the gas tank. But Dumphee couldn't find it anywhere.

A little man with beady eyes watched Dumphee from a bulletproof gas booth, and after several minutes he came out.

"What the hell kind of vehicle is that?" he asked, his mustache twitching. He went and peered through the windshield to an ID plate on the dashboard, then read, "XM-666-AST—Am . . . Amphibious Swamp Truck."

Trying to be helpful, the fellow blurted, "Hey, you know, on some of these new cars and whatnot, they hide the gas tanks. Makes it harder for the thieves, I guess."

The attendant rushed around the back of the vehicle, pulled down the license plate. Sure enough, there was the gas tank.

The attendant glanced at the gas intake. "Just like the Army. No one else in the country can use leaded gas on new vehicles but the government."

He set the gas nozzle into the hole, began pumping and rushed round to his bulletproof booth for the next customer. Dumphee watched the meter on the tank for a long time. When it reached a hundred gallons, the attendant shouted at him, "Hey, buddy, you're taking my whole reserves!"

At a hundred and twenty gallons, the tank filled. Dumphee hung the nozzle back on the pump, got the military gas vouchers from the lieutenant, who said, "Make sure you get twenty in change."

Dumphee didn't know what he was talking about. The gas vouchers looked like huge checks, with three layers of carbon forms and a plastic credit card that had to be imprinted on the forms in order for them to be used. Most gas station attendants blew a gasket just looking at the things, not knowing how to use them. But they were only good for gas purchases. You couldn't get change from them.

But when he went to the booth, the attendant said, "How much change do you want?"

"Uh, twenty," Dumphee said.

The fellow expertly filled in the voucher, ran the card through the machine to imprint the form, had Dumphee sign the slips. The attendant had added $40 in "gas" to the sale. He handed Dumphee twenty in change and gave him a wink.

When Dumphee got back to the truck, Lieutenant Fugg grabbed the twenty from him and said, "Now, keep your eyes open for a McDonald's."

Dumphee started the swamp truck and floated it out onto the highway, looking for a McDonald's.

On the freeway, he saw a gray sedan with tinted windows heading east suddenly veer, do a U-turn, and head back toward him.

This wasn't a good sign; he began thinking of Russian spies.

In the driving rain, he pulled off the freeway and turned down a country road.

He hit the gas, hoping that if he got far enough ahead of the gray sedan, he'd lose it.

He glanced at Fugg. The lieutenant had closed his eyes and seemed unaware that Dumphee was going in the wrong direction.

I'm probably scared of nothing, Dumphee told himself. There really aren't any Russian spies behind me. He cranked up the engine. The ATV topped out at ninety-five miles an hour.

Dumphee glanced up at the map shining on his windshield. The narrow road he was on went on into Pittsburgh. In the rearview mirror, he couldn't see any headlights speeding toward him. Yet he suspected that the sedan might be there, sliding through the darkness like a shark beneath a wine-dark sea.

He reached down to the *Armaments* button on the dashboard, thought of pressing it, of getting ready for an attack. But what if that's just some civilian car, and I blow it up? he wondered. His finger hovered over the button.

Use the Force, Dumphee, he thought. Let go. Trust your feelings. Oh, this is dumb, he concluded.

He suddenly wondered if this truck had a radio, and studied the dashboard for a moment. A little music might help distract him, calm his racing heart. The ATV had an altimeter, gauges to show the air pressure in all six tires, gauges for oil, coolant, engine temperature, transmission fluid, battery charge. But no radio. At least nothing but a military communications set, which wouldn't pick up FM.

Dumphee remembered the Sony Walkman in his duffel bag, pulled it out, put the headphones over his ears and flipped the radio on.

Futuristic rock came pounding from the speakers. He tried tuning to a bluegrass station—through some oldies channels— found Wagner's "Ride of the Valkyries" blaring.

Ahead he saw the friendly golden arches of a McDonald's. He glanced in his rearview mirror.

By the light of an oncoming car he thought he saw a flash of gray and chrome. His heart hammered. As he passed a streetlight, he saw clearly the gray sedan streaking up behind him, headlights off.

Dumphee jabbed a finger into the vehicle's *Armaments* button, and the machine gun rose into view. But mounted as it was on the front right fender, it couldn't swivel back and fire at something behind—not without blowing a hole big enough for a 'coon to scramble through right in Dumphee's chest. It only worked as a forward gun.

He pressed a button to arm the right rear missile tube. A computerized voice said, "Missile armed and searching for target."

He pressed the *Fire* button.

The computerized voice said, "Searching for enemy transponder frequencies. No enemy planes or tanks within a thirty-mile radius. Missile disengaged."

"Hell," Dumphee shouted at the stupid ATV, hoping that the voice recognition chip would understand. "There's a car right behind us! Blow that sucker up!"

The gray sedan veered left, as if to pass at a hundred miles per hour, and Dumphee saw the gray-tinted windows sliding down as the sedan began to draw even with him. A fellow pointed a machine gun out the window, and Dumphee realized that he didn't have so much as a rock handy to throw in self-defense.

He screamed loud enough to wake Fugg.

Dumphee dropped his Walkman, grabbed the wheel in both hands, hit the brakes and banked hard to the left, slamming his front fender into the sedan. The sedan went spinning into the oncoming lane.

Suddenly the ATV was hurtling off the road, two wheels on the sidewalk, speeding toward the McDonald's. The headlights played through the restaurant, shining on a playland filled with purple tunnels and nets. As the lights hit the front door, a fellow walking out the entrance dropped a breakfast roll and coffee.

We're going to hit! Dumphee thought. We're going to smash all them poor waitresses flatter than Egg McMuffins!

The tires squealed as the vehicle spun out of control. The big round wheels hit a speed bump in the parking lot. There was a rattle and a crash in the cargo hold, and Dumphee's forehead slammed into the steering wheel.

CHAPTER 5

When Dumphee opened his eyes, a brilliant tangerine fog surrounded the truck, and the tang of ozone hung heavy in the air. The vehicle rolled through the odd vapors until gradually the fog dissipated. Dumphee cut the engine and just stared.

"What the hell?" Fugg cried, rousing from his slumber. He could not have failed to hear the smashing of vehicles, the squealing of tires, Dumphee's shouts. "We at McDonald's yet?"

Full sunlight streamed through the sky as the truck wheeled through the narrow street of a town. Log buildings hunkered close. Around the buildings, a stockade rose some twenty feet high, wooden pickets on the fence.

The Walkman on the floor issued only static.

"Oh, hell," Dumphee said. "We triggered that time machine!"

He jumped from the vehicle and found himself standing knee-deep in foul-smelling mud. A town squatted around him. A small tavern and trading post lay just to his right, smoke roiling from their chimneys. Old Indian squaws and trappers tended cooking fires beside the wall of a barracks, where beaver and mink furs on stretching poles hung by the hundreds. Several dogs ran through the streets, yapping at a fat trapper on a mule that kicked wildly.

Everyone on the street suddenly turned to look at Dumphee's vehicle, gaping in surprise.

Somewhere, a gun fired. Dumphee cringed, afraid that he was the target.

In the cab of the ATV, Lieutenant Fugg shouted, "Hey, this isn't McDonald's! Where the hell are we?"

Dumphee gulped, heart hammering, not quite sure what to answer. Somewhere a military drum was pounding.

Up the street he heard giggling. Several young Indian women had been sitting with some old squaws in the shade outside of a barracks. Now the women began to run toward Dumphee, laughing and pointing.

One young woman at the head of the group was tall, beautiful and stately, perhaps eighteen. She had raven hair, generous breasts and the dark eyes of a doe. She was dressed in beaded buckskins that were worn and a bit dirty.

The maidens with her were shorter.

All the Indian maidens rushed up to him. Dumphee could only stand, mouth agape, as they giggled and studied him. It was not until they were nearly on him that he noticed their smell—rancid fat, dirt and dog hair.

The girls held their hands over their mouths and tittered like shy birds, pointing at the gold-colored buttons on his dress uniform, at his ATV.

The tall one said to the others, "Shhhh, shhhh. He English soldier."

She stepped forward, thrusting her chest out in an exaggerated pose, as if to show her bravery, and edged close to Dumphee. She said loudly, "My name Lotsa Smoke. I heap big English woman. My father Pierre Beaucoup, bigges' Frenchman in all Canada." She held her arms out wide, as if to hold Canada in them.

"No she not," one of the other Indian girls tittered. "She jus' Mohawk squaw, like rest of us."

Lotsa Smoke covered her mouth with her hand and giggled. "That right."

Another young woman slipped from behind Lotsa Smoke. "Me Sees Far," she introduced herself, squinting up into his face.

Sees Far, Dumphee thought, not close.

Then all the women began shouting their names, "Me Pretty Rose." "Me Far Walk." "Me Bear Tail."

By this time, Lieutenant Fugg had climbed down from the truck. He shouted, "Private, where in the hell did you take us?"

37

"Oh, look," one of the maidens cried, pointing at the lieutenant. "They *both* got gold buttons." The next thing Dumphee knew, the Indian girl was pulling at his buttons, fingering his shirt. Several others joined in. Some hands grabbed his biceps, as if to check for muscles, others stroked him seductively.

Dumphee stumbled back against the fender of the truck, climbed up on it, then climbed to the hood to get away. A couple of the maidens moved toward Fugg as he came around the front of the ATV.

Fugg simply leered broadly at the Indian women, and said, "Yeah, solid gold buttons, ladies—just like my tooth." He flashed a smile wide enough to show his golden molar, and spread his arms wide in invitation. "Come on over here, sweet things. I'll treat you ladies to some fries if you'll point me toward a McDonald's."

A couple of women looked at him strangely and began asking among themselves, "McDonald's? McDonald's?"

Whereas they had been brazen toward Dumphee, they could not help but see the intent in Fugg's eyes. Some of them suddenly became shy while others swarmed to him. In a moment, he had a couple of willing maidens under each arm. They looked at him admiringly while they fingered his gold buttons.

Lotsa Smoke grabbed Bear Tail and pushed her toward the fort. "Get Macdonald!" she shouted. Bear Tail took off running.

Now that the Mohawk women had calmed, Dumphee stepped away from the truck to study his surroundings better.

He was still in shock, wondering what to do now, how to get back to his own time.

Fugg smiled broadly. "So, are we on a movie set, or something? Where you ladies from?" He stared pointedly at Lotsa Smoke's ample bosom and crooned, "Man, do I love your Silicon Valley."

"Uh, Lieutenant," Dumphee said, realizing that Fugg had somehow not yet figured out what had happened. "I got something to tell you."

"Not now," Fugg said, pushing him aside as he made his way to Lotsa Smoke.

In a moment Bear Tail returned, leading a Scotsman in a kilt, who limped quickly after. His leg was splinted. A white bandage wrapped about his head was stained red with blood, which had seeped down the side of his face and dried. He wore an expression so sour that as Dumphee's grandma would have said, "It could curdle lemonade."

The Scotsman hobbled up to Fugg. "Here now," he said in a thick brogue, "I'm Macdonald. I hear you been callin' after me. Who in the name o' Beelzebub might you be?" He studied the ATV suspiciously for half a heartbeat, "And what might you be doin' with a teepee on wheels?"

Dumphee halfway came to attention. "Uh, he's Lieutenant Fugg, of the United States Army, and I'm Private, Third Class, Dumphee." Dumphee didn't like the way this dour old man was looking at his vehicle. "I hope you don't mind if we park here."

Suddenly there was a burst of gunfire from above the gates. Fugg nearly threw himself down in panic. Macdonald eyed Fugg critically. "Soldier? He calls hisself a soldier? I wouldna 'ave a mule that was so gun-shy!"

"Wait a minute!" Fugg shouted, suddenly looking all about, reappraising the situation. "Where the hell am I?"

Macdonald grinned. "'Hell.' That's as good a name for it as any. You're at Fort Pitt, of course. We're under siege, mon! Pontiac has stirred up every tribe in the west. It's a fewking row! It's been so all July!"

Fugg glanced down at his watch. "It's not July. It's September!"

"Why, you're mad, mon!" Macdonald barked.

"Uh, Mr. Macdonald, sir," Dumphee said, trying to cover for Fugg. "Lieutenant Fugg is a bit disoriented—he, uh, took a bump to the head. Enemy tomahawk."

Another soldier fired from the wall, and Fugg ducked again. Macdonald gave him a hard glare, as if even a head wound were no excuse for cowardice.

Fugg began shaking his watch. "You know, I think my watch stopped."

"It's Pontiac that's got to be stopped," Macdonald growled. "And forget about your head, mon. If you think you've got it bad now, try gettin' yerself scalped." He pointed to his own bandaged head.

"Ow," Lieutenant Fugg said, studying the bandage in sympathy. "That does look like it hurts!"

Fugg's face suddenly brightened, as if he'd just realized that someone was playing a joke on him. "So, you got scalped, and now you and your Klingon girls here want help from the United Federation of Planets?"

"Klingons?" Macdonald asked. He explained loudly and patiently, as if to someone who was deaf or mentally deficient, "No, mon, you've got the wrong tribe. These is Mohawks. Friendlies. Pro-English. They was captured out of a Quaker Missionary School by them varmints that's attacking us—the Mingoes. But then some of Johnson's Iroquois captured them back. So now they're Iroquois slaves. They belong to them old women over there by the cooking pots."

He waved toward some old squaws who were sitting on the ground, gnawing at leather to soften it with their teeth. The cooking pots were big iron cauldrons, sitting on tripods, like something a witch might use to boil children in.

Macdonald continued, "But forget the squaws for now. Ye wouldna have a coin or two, would ye, lad? For if ye have, ye could buy me a wee dram. . . ."

Fugg was still busy admiring the "Klingons," so Dumphee reached into his pocket and tossed a couple of Kennedy half dollars to Macdonald. He figured that anyone who'd been scalped probably needed a good stiff drink.

Macdonald grabbed the coins in midair and eyed them for a moment, turning them on edge until he could see the copper. "Counterfeit," he muttered darkly, tossing them to the dirt. He gave Dumphee a long, evil glare, then turned and stumped away.

Lotsa Smoke knelt and studied the coins, then held one up to her neck admiringly, as if it were a pendant on a necklace. Her dark eyes shone when she looked at Dumphee.

Fugg said, "Say, I'm hungry. Where can we get something to eat around here?"

Lotsa Smoke stared at Dumphee as she answered, eyes full of admiration. "Our owners. They feed, if you pay." She nodded toward the old squaws who tended the cooking pots.

"Yeah, I'll pay," Fugg said absently. He was grinning at Sees Far, who smiled back shyly as he draped an arm around her. A little glue in the right places would have cemented their relationship.

Fugg pulled the twenty-dollar bill out of his pocket, handed it to Dumphee. "Go get us something."

"Uh, Lieutenant Fugg," Dumphee said, "we've got to have a talk." Fugg was still admiring the maidens, but began to seem confused, as if it were dawning on him that something odd had happened. "We have to talk *now!*"

"Yeah, Dumphee?" Fugg asked.

"Do you remember what we were carrying in the ATV?"

Fugg's face scrunched up in concentration. "Was it . . . I remember something about Russian weapons. Experimental weapons?"

"That's part of the load. But the main thing was a *time machine*. I think it went off. . . ."

"You mean . . . ?" Fugg's eyes widened. "You mean we're stuck back in time? Back here?" Fugg looked up the wall, saw a redcoat with a tamping rod trying to reload his musket, and looked at the Indian maidens. "And we've got"—Fugg began to think faster, and suddenly he grinned and his whole demeanor changed—"two modern soldiers with enough weapons in the back of our truck so we can *take over the world?*"

"I guess so, maybe. . . ." Dumphee said, not liking Fugg's tone.

"Well!" Fugg said thoughtfully. "Well, well, well! Why don't you go get us some lunch while I think a little more about this . . . opportunity for promotion."

Dumphee took the money and cringed.

Lotsa Smoke led Dumphee down the street toward the old squaws. As Dumphee left, he heard Fugg tell Sees Far, "You really like these gold buttons, don't you? Maybe we ought to find someplace private, and you could show me what you'll give for them."

Dumphee shot him a cold glare, but Fugg didn't notice. He was too interested in finding out what he could get from Sees Far.

Dumphee wasn't interested in taking over the world—especially since it was obvious that Fugg, as senior officer, would be in charge. Dumphee didn't doubt that Fugg could wreak some major havoc.

It wouldn't take much to duplicate the modern weapons—grenades, revolvers, bazookas. It would be all the easier with the truck filled with some of the better examples of modern weaponry.

When Dumphee looked back at Fugg, he recalled one of his pappy's favorite expressions: "Power tends to corrupt and absolute power corrupts absolutely."

While they walked, Lotsa Smoke watched Dumphee constantly from the corner of her eyes, a secretive smile on her lips. Pretty Rose and Bear Tail followed a step behind.

As Dumphee approached the cooking pots, one old woman tossed dried meat into the pot. She didn't look up until he overshadowed her, then she asked, "Qui le sacre bleu est vous?" Who the hell are you?

Dumphee knew French when he heard it, and suddenly he wished once again that he were civilized, that he knew how to order at French restaurants. The stew smelled delicious. The small flames from the fire licked at Dumphee's boots. He could see potatoes and yams, garlic and meat floating in the kettle.

"I, uh, don't speak French very well," Dumphee said. He tried talking slowly, hoping that he'd be able to communicate. "But these women," he pointed to Lotsa Smoke and the others, "they say you might sell—"

"Here, I tell them," Lotsa Smoke said, and she began speaking rapidly in French, gesturing toward Dumphee. She finished speaking, and the squaw's eyes widened.

The old squaws stared hard at Dumphee, uncomprehending. Their eyes roamed over the gold buttons on his dress uniform, then over his insignia and pins, until one of them noticed his army belt buckle flashing golden in the sunlight.

"Yi!" the old squaw shouted. "Gol'!"

She reached out as if to paw the belt buckle, then glanced at the three maidens behind Dumphee, her eyes wide with cupidity.

The old woman seemed unable to contain herself any longer. With a screech she leapt over the tripod and kettle, slamming into Dumphee, knocking him backward. Then five other old squaws were after him.

Dumphee was so startled, he couldn't think what to do. He wondered if he'd insulted the old woman, and began to retreat, stepping backward, but tripped on something—Lotsa Smoke's foot. He hit the mud, landing on his back.

The old squaws leapt on him and began ripping off his buttons and buckle, shouting in French, *"Or buttones! Or buttones! Or buttones!"*

Dumphee tried to hold up the twenty-dollar bill to placate the women, and shouted, "Hey—don't—rip" *(grunt)* "my—uniform!"

Lotsa Smoke shouted at the old squaws in French, tried to pull one away. But the women tore at Dumphee's remaining buttons and pulled off his insignia. Dumphee tried to push one squaw off, but she wrestled his arm down and stepped on it in a very businesslike fashion while Dumphee squirmed in the mud.

Why, Dumphee thought, these women are as hot to get my clothes off as Jo Beth is after a couple of beers!

In thirty seconds the old squaws had removed all his buttons and insignia, then they ran off in a pack—squabbling over who was going to get the belt buckle.

Dumphee rolled up to one elbow, shaking his head, studying his uniform. "Man, if the MPs saw me now, they'd lock me up for a 'coon's age."

He yelled at the old squaws. "Hey, don't I at least get some food?"

One squaw on the porch turned, stared at him with narrowed eyes, listening thoughtfully.

"Food! Food! Can I have some food?" Dumphee made shoveling motions toward his mouth.

"Ugh," she pointed at the pot. "You buy. Squaws yours."

"No. *Food!* I want food!" Dumphee said.

The squaw looked down at the buttons, as if she rued the bargain, "Food yours, too." She nodded slightly, then turned away and began to hurry off.

"N———!" Dumphee began to shout, just as Lotsa Smoke grabbed him and yanked him to his feet, and started to brush off his clothes.

"Oh," Lotsa Smoke said gratefully, cutting him off. "Oh! Thank you for buying us. Old squaws very mean to us. But we good squaws. Make you very happy. Thank you! Thank you! We get ready come with you now!"

Lotsa Smoke, Pretty Rose and Bear Tail turned and sprinted off toward the nearest barracks.

"Wait!" Dumphee yelled, trying to clear things up. But the girls ignored him and as he watched them run, he got to thinking: He'd just freed some slaves. He hadn't meant to, but that's what he'd done, and he didn't regret it. The old squaws were mean to the younger maidens, and Lotsa Smoke's tone told him that Dumphee had just made her day.

Three women for two dollars' worth of army buttons?

No matter how you sliced it, that was a bargain.

And Lotsa Smoke was so good looking, Dumphee would have been too intimidated to ask her for a date back home.

And if Dumphee set these women free, it would be kind of like rescuing them. Of course, he wouldn't set them free right away. He'd want to keep them a day or two, just to get to know them. And that Lotsa Smoke spoke French and Mohawk and English and probably some other languages, and she might be no end of help to him while he tried to figure out how to get back home.

Dumphee stared after them, and slowly began wiping the mud from his hands and legs, looking at his messy clothes. He stared longingly at the food. An iron ladle was in the stewpot, and several clay bowls painted with bright Indian designs lay upside down beside the pot.

He didn't know if he should take the bowls—partly because they looked like valuable antiques, and partly because they were so dirty he didn't think anyone ought to ever eat from one again.

He was disturbed by the sound of a drumbeat, and turned to see twenty redcoats marching up the street, their flintlock rifles at their shoulders, long bayonets pointing at the sun. Macdonald was marching with them, and some drummer boy. The look of rage in Macdonald's eyes was hard to miss.

Dumphee realized he wanted to put something between himself and this madman. So Dumphee began edging toward the ATV.

"There he is!" Macdonald shouted at the commanding officer. "The counterfeiter! Get him!"

The commander of the squadron drew his sword in one smooth motion and shouted to his men: "Muskets, pike position! Squooohaaad, charge!"

CHAPTER 6

The drummer boy beat the charge, and the soldiers lowered their bayonets. Macdonald rushed in front of the soldiers, pointing an accusatory finger at Dumphee. Only the scalped man standing between those soldiers and Dumphee kept them from shooting.

Dumphee didn't wait to see what happened next. He rushed for the ATV, shouting, "Lieutenant Fugg!"

Fugg was nowhere to be seen—until Dumphee spotted him near the corner of a building with Sees Far. He was passionately kissing her cheek and whispering in her ear. With one hand, he groped at her breast, but his head pulled back a bit as Dumphee yelled, "Lieutenant, let's get out of here! The redcoats are coming!"

Hearing grunts and shouts, Dumphee turned to see some soldiers lower to their knees, ready to shoot. But at that moment, Lotsa Smoke and the other young squaws raced in front of them, spoiling the soldiers' chance for a shot. Lotsa Smoke had grabbed the cooking pot from the tripod and was rushing toward Dumphee. Each woman carried a deer hide, with clothes and whatnot rolled inside.

"Lieutenant Fugg!" Dumphee shouted as he raced for the ATV.

With a roar, the soldiers jumped back up, giving chase with shouts of "For King George!"

Dumphee flung open the door to the ATV and leapt in.

He tried to slam the door shut, but a soldier raced up behind and latched on to it. Another brought a bayonet down from above, and Dumphee dodged right. The bayonet slashed into the upholstery by his shoulder.

Dumphee hit the ignition.

The engine roared to life. The soldier holding the door yelped in terror at the engine's growl and fell back. Dumphee slammed the door closed and locked it, then three soldiers were scrabbling over the hood, glaring at him through the windshield. Another grabbed the far door.

Dumphee threw the rig into reverse, twisted the wheel to the left, and was gratified to see the soldiers go flying off the hood with astonished expressions.

The soldier on the far door began cursing as he fumbled with the latch. When he got it to work, the door swung farther open, throwing him to the ground.

Dumphee shouted again in frustration, "Lieutenant!" He looked in the rearview mirror.

Instead of rushing toward him, Fugg ducked behind the barracks. Apparently he felt that whatever trouble Dumphee had gotten into, Fugg didn't want to be a part of it.

In that moment, blinded by panic and a sense of betrayal, Dumphee decided to leave him. Leave him alone and weaponless here in this danged fort and never come back. Fugg was too untrustworthy.

Ahead of the truck, several soldiers dropped to their knees and prepared to fire.

Dumphee hit the gas and ducked his head below the dashboard. He whispered a small prayer of thanks to the Army driving school as he employed his dodge-and-drive skills. He'd fixed the position of the troops in his mind, and now he raced toward that spot, hoping to scare them.

The passenger door was still open. Two soldiers rushed to get in.

Then, suddenly, Lotsa Smoke raced up behind them, swinging the iron pot like it was a morningstar, knocking both soldiers aside. She dove into the seat beside Dumphee.

Dumphee heard terrified shouts from the squadron of soldiers, and a gun discharged, smoke puffing up from its barrel.

Lotsa smoke raised her head to look over the dashboard, eyes shining with ecstasy. "Whee!" she cried.

"No! Not *whee!*" Dumphee said, pulling her head down just as another musket fired. A musket ball pierced the windshield, hit a metal brace, and bounced onto the floor of the cab.

Dumphee reached past Lotsa Smoke, pulled the passenger door closed and locked it. Then quickly peeked up through the windshield.

The ATV was hurtling toward a barricade of barrels, piled atop one another. The stockade gates lay beyond. Soldiers were springing from the truck's path, falling sprawled into the mud. Two men at the stockade gates seemed torn between running away and opening the gates to let this metal monster out.

Pretty Rose and Bear Tail raced after the truck, trying to reach it, dismay showing in their faces. Dumphee hit the brakes, slowing enough so that they could catch up. They tossed their bundles in the back and dived into the bed of the ATV.

Pretty Rose shouted, "Okay, go fast!"

The truck hit the barricade of piled barrels. Water gushed from the lowest barrels, while the upper ones rolled onto the hood and were thrown aside.

Dumphee heard Indian war whoops from the back of the truck. He looked up over the wheel and pointed the vehicle toward the fortress gates, hoping the guards would let him pass.

One guard dove aside, but the other kept his nerve and raised a hand, palm outward, shouting, "Halt!"

Dumphee started to hit the brakes, but looked up to his left. On the wall-walk, a soldier had wrestled a cannon around so that it pointed at his ATV. He held a long glowing taper in his hand, and was about to ignite the cannon's fuse.

Dumphee considered the *Armaments* button, glowing redly on his dashboard. He decided against it.

Instead, he honked his horn and hit the gas. The sentry leapt aside as the ATV hit the stockade gate. The pounding from the truck was so terrible, that the cannoneer and his little platform swayed in the air, just as the cannon blew.

The shot went high and wide, hitting a henhouse inside the compound. The whole thing exploded in red fury, sending shards of wood from the henhouse flying a hundred feet into the air. Dead chickens suddenly rained from the sky.

Dumphee crashed through the gates and hit the accelerator.

The squaws began shouting, "Woo haw! Hee! Heee!"

Then he was hurtling along a rutted dirt road toward a broad river. The ATV hit the water with a huge splash, and from the fortress behind, Dumphee heard the crackle of musket fire. He looked in his rearview mirror. Redcoats manned the walls of the fort, puffs of smoke rising from their guns.

Musket balls began plunking in the water around the truck. One squaw in back of the truck screamed, a horrible wail.

"She shot!" Lotsa Smoke yelled.

Dumphee looked back. The truck sped over the water, and in the back of the truck bed, guns and ammo cases had spilled all over everything. Bear Tail held her stomach, shouting in pain and dismay, "Oh! Oh! Oh! Oh! Oh! Oh!"

"What—were you hit?" Dumphee cried.

She pulled something away from her stomach. "My looking glass broke! You owe me new one!"

Dumphee stared into a broken mirror.

Pretty Rose teased, "Oh, that okay Bear Tail; you so ugly, maybe better if you not look in mirrors anyway."

Suddenly the bullets quit firing from the fort. The ATV had moved out of the gunmen's range.

CHAPTER 7

In the silence that followed, Dumphee began to take stock of the situation. What am I doing? Dumphee wondered. He'd just escaped the fort, but now that he considered it, leaving Lieutenant Fugg behind seemed . . . impetuous. They were fellow soldiers after all. Dumphee would just have to go back to the fort and get him.

But that would be damned near impossible, what with wild Mingoes out here. Besides, if Dumphee drove back, the redcoats would shoot as soon as he got near.

"Oh boy, I hope they didn't get my license number," he muttered. He tried to imagine sneaking back into the fort without the ATV, but that seemed foolhardy.

For several long minutes, the swamp truck rolled down the river. Dumphee stuck his head out, looked back toward the fort.

The bank was rolling by quickly, and Dumphee realized that the current was pushing them along. He cut the engine while he considered his options.

"Let's watch for a bridge," he said after some thought. "That will mean there's a town nearby, where we can get food."

"You hungry?" Lotsa Smoke asked. She lifted the black stewpot from the floor, reached in with her hands and fished out a piece of meat—a rib bone. She handed it to Dumphee.

He began chewing it thoughtfully.

The countryside they floated past was wild and beautiful. Pussy willows along the river were still green in midsummer, and the leaves on the cottonwoods were thick and full. They passed a family of deer that had bedded by the water. A huge buck just stood and stared at them, its horns still in velvet.

Ahead, a mother mallard and her chicks swam out of the willows to look at the truck, then she quacked and swam back into the brush.

Dumphee glanced in the rearview mirror. Pretty Rose and Bear Tail each sat near the back of the truck, letting their hands idly trail in the water.

Dumphee leaned his head back, sweat pouring down his forehead, and just closed his eyes a minute, thinking furiously. Lieutenant Fugg was still in the fort.

Dumphee wondered if he should try to rescue him. But he didn't know Fugg well, and certainly didn't trust him. Fugg had walked the other way when Dumphee called for help, and the man's first thought upon learning that they were stuck in the past was that this might prove a fine opportunity to take over the world.

He isn't just untrustworthy, he's dangerous, Dumphee decided. And if I do go back and risk my life to save him—even if I manage to get us both out of Fort Pitt alive—I'd just have to fight him somewhere down the line.

It's better to just let sleeping dogs lie, Dumphee told himself, no matter how hard it is.

Hell—he soothed his conscience with this thought—at least Fugg has enough "gold" buttons to buy himself a wife. He'll have Sees Far to entertain him. Someday, six months from now, he might wake up and wish for a flush toilet and a television.

But Dumphee felt pretty sure that otherwise Fugg would be fine.

Yet Dumphee felt a niggling concern about leaving a man back in time. He'd seen enough TV to know that he had to start worrying about the space-time continuum. You couldn't just leave a man from the future in the past.

What if Fugg accidentally killed his own grandfather? He'd never be born.

Well, that obviously hadn't happened. More likely, with the way Fugg had been eyeing Sees Far, he *was* his own grandfather.

Maybe he'd just stay here and breed. His line would go on from generation to generation, until Lieutenant Fugg was born and went back in time. Then the whole cycle would start all over again.

Well, if that was the worst that would happen, then Dumphee wouldn't feel bad about leaving Fugg.

Dumphee squinted, picked up his little Sony Walkman off the floor and flipped it back on. Only static came from it. Radios won't be invented for two hundred years, he realized.

"What year is it?" he asked. He knew those muskets had been old models. Before 1800. But he didn't know how much older they might be.

Lotsa Smoke just shrugged.

Pretty Rose said, "Is year 1132, and you just got back from Crusades. I think Saracens hit you in head with piece of True Cross, very hard."

Dumphee ignored her joke, realizing that the diminutive squaw must think he was dumb or crazy.

"Man, I'm an awful long way from home. . . ." he whispered.

"Home? Where home?" Lotsa Smoke asked.

"A little place. French Creek, West Virginia."

Lotsa Smoke nodded appreciatively. "Oh, you lucky you French. Pontiac and Mingoes, they fight for French. If you not French, they take scalp quicky-quick. We squaws be very lucky be married to Frenchman. Mingoes all down this river. . . ."

She suddenly squinted at Dumphee slyly, began rattling something off in French, "Que" something or other. Dumphee didn't have to know French to know what she asked.

"No, you're right, I don't speak French."

"Oh," she said, crestfallen.

Pretty Rose laughed, "Then maybe we all gonna die."

"Not if I can help it," Dumphee said. He glanced up at the map that shone on what was left of his windshield. A musket ball had pierced one corner of it. According to the map, he was driving between some skyscrapers in downtown Pittsburgh.

"You know," Dumphee said when he finished gnawing the meat off his bone, "this is pretty good. What is it?"

Lotsa Smoke smiled broadly, happy to please him. "Dog. The very best."

"Dog?" Dumphee asked in horror.

Lotsa Smoke reached into the pot and grabbed some more.

"Oh yes, good dog. No tough like coyote. This very good dog." She held up a leg bone for Dumphee, but when he didn't take it quickly, she smacked her lips and bit off a little for herself.

Stomach revolting at the thought, Dumphee turned away. Lotsa Smoke was a beautiful woman, but even he couldn't sit here and watch her eat a dog.

He noticed a log poking up out of the water ahead and turned the wheel so that the rudders would veer the truck from its course.

He felt something on the back of his hand. A huge louse crawled up from under his shirt, rested on his knuckle. In horror, he flicked it against the inside of the windshield and glanced back to Lotsa Smoke.

She stared at him with wide, innocent eyes, chewing the dog leg. A huge louse crawled from her scalp toward her ear. Two smaller ones crawled up from her collar onto her neck.

Lotsa Smoke kept eating, never noticing the insects.

"You know, you're a beautiful woman," Dumphee said thoughtfully. "But you've got bugs!"

He reached over and grabbed a big louse that was heading down her neck toward her cleavage. "I'll tell you what: the first island we come to . . ." he looked ahead, saw the gravel bar of an island in the distance, then fired up the engine and started toward it. "I'm going to let you get out and take a bath. All of you!"

——

Dumphee pulled the truck onto a spit of sandy gravel on the upstream end of the island. The afternoon sunlight slanted into the woods, not quite penetrating the shadows. Birches and deeper woods lay beyond. Here in the sun, he figured, would be the perfect spot for the girls to bathe. The inside cut of the river was deep, the water clear. He could see a couple of big trout sunning in the water, snapping at flies. Big native brown trout. He wished he had his pappy here, with his fly rod.

He pulled the truck up to the shore, then got out and stood on the beach. "All right, you!" he shouted like a first sergeant. "If you're going to ride in this truck, you're going to have to take a bath. So into the water! All three of you! Now! Now! Now!"

The squaws stared at him as if they'd never heard of bathing.

"I mean it!" Dumphee said, hoping to get the idea across. "Into the water, and take your clothes off!"

Lotsa Smoke smiled at the other two, said something in Mohawk, and all three women jumped him.

Dumphee didn't have a chance. Those Indian squaws were stronger than any women he'd ever met back home, and they wriggled about like professional Jello wrestlers. With his belt and buttons already gone, they shucked his clothes down to his underwear in no time. The next thing he knew, the women were giggling and screaming as they carried him through the air, then tossed him into the deepest part of the river.

He came up sputtering.

Lotsa Smoke and the others climbed in on top of him, pushing his head under. The women all screamed and laughed.

CHAPTER 8

Half an hour later, Dumphee squatted on the beach in his underwear, the tails of his shirt trailing in the sand. He'd found some MREs, "Meals, Ready to Eat," in back of the truck. Now he pried them open.

He glanced up at Lotsa Smoke. The squaws were only half dressed in buckskins and little breast-bands. The sun was drying their naked skin. Lotsa Smoke shot Dumphee a fetching grin as she combed out her long dark hair.

Dumphee saw the little leather bag where she kept her combs and whatnot. Two big lice crawled from the bag onto Lotsa Smoke's bare leg and began making their way toward her scalp.

"Well, it was worth a try," he grumbled.

Just then, he finished prying the top off the MREs. He looked inside, his stomach flipping a little at the very thought.

"Hey, look," he apologized, "I ain't got many MREs, and they're awful anyway. You girls got anything to eat—that isn't dog, that is?"

Pretty Rose came up to his side, glanced at the MREs, and lowered to her haunches, gazing at the food thoughtfully. She sniffed the can and made a face in disgust. "You eat this? You must be heap brave. If you think this better than dog, maybe you not smart. When you child, did mule kick you in head?"

Bear Tail leapt up, shouting, "Look! Ooooh—look!"

Upriver, a small herd of buffalo had come down to the edge of the water, and now they began swimming across.

"I spot buffalo for you. Now you owe me two mirrors!" Bear Tail shouted in triumph.

With a whoop, she rushed to the back of the truck, came back with Dumphee's M-16 and a bag full of clips.

"No! Wait a minute!" Dumphee said.

Bear Tail struck a pose, aiming the rifle. "You heap big brave. You shoot."

"Now, wait a minute," Dumphee said. "Where I come from, these critters are an *endangered species.*"

"Not endangered species—these good buffalo. You shoot! We eat!" Bear Tail shouted. She shoved him in the chest with the gun, knocking him back.

Dumphee wondered again about the space-time continuum. If he shot a buffalo, how many buffalo would disappear down the line?

But the women had to eat, and they wanted buffalo.

Dumphee raised the gun, thinking, Man, I'm glad Judge Wright isn't here to see this. He took aim at the herd leader, which was halfway across the river now, the shaggy black hump of its back bobbing on the water.

Dumphee squeezed the trigger. Thirty shots sprayed from the barrel, blowing the animal into coarse chunks. Whatever might happen down the time line, this one buffalo was decidedly extinct.

Dumphee squinted at his target. "There you go, ladies: buffalo burger!"

No one answered. He looked to his side, carefully. The squaws had all disappeared, were nowhere in sight.

Dumphee heard a squeaking noise of terror to his left. Lotsa Smoke, Bear Tail and Pretty Rose had all dived behind a log. They stared at him with eyes wide, terrified.

"Hey, I'm sorry," Dumphee said. "I had it on full auto."

Lotsa Smoke got up from behind the log, half covered in old leaves, and walked toward Dumphee very slowly, her face a study in awe. She carefully examined the weapon in Dumphee's hands, reached out and touched it, stroking the barrel.

She took a deep breath and stood tall. "Heap great war chief!" she said, staring up at Dumphee.

Dumphee smiled at her appreciatively. "Honey, you don't know how great."

She turned and began shouting at the other women in Mohawk. In half a moment, Bear Tail and Pretty Rose jumped in the water and began swimming upriver.

"They bring. They bring the meat!" Lotsa Smoke said.

⊤⊤⊤⊤⊤

Far downstream, two Seneca braves heard the cracking sound of gunfire. The sound of many redcoats. They squatted beside the river, staring about, faces masked in war paint, until the oldest one, a chief, reached into the water with the barrel of his flintlock rifle and fished out a piece of paper.

He held it up for inspection. The other grabbed it and studied the sheets of carbon-backed paper that shredded in his hand, mystified. The gasoline receipt.

In contempt, the Seneca chief ground the paper into the mud beneath his heel. The chief crouched low, glaring upriver. His warrior turned and raced deep into the woods.

CHAPTER 9

In the twilight, Dumphee sorted through his duffel bag, studying its contents and wondering. He still didn't know what all he had in the truck. The squaws had searched the back and found some kind of experimental Russian commando knives that were almost as big as machetes. The blades on them had some kind of grains embedded in the metal— maybe green diamonds. The heavy blades were so sharp, they could probably slice through protective body armor like it was toilet paper.

Two squaws chopped down saplings with the huge knives, then sliced off bark to tie the sticks together to form drying racks. A fire burned low at the edge of the camp, and Dumphee had pulled the truck close to it.

The squaws dragged the dead buffalo up to the riverbank.

Dumphee wondered. He figured that a little jiggling of that time machine had sent him back a couple of hundred years. What would happen if he kicked it big time? Would he find himself out here with the Romans or something?

The old cave preacher up at Blue Grouse Creek said that the earth was only six thousand years old. Dumphee doubted it. But if it were true, Dumphee could go back and maybe see the face of God himself.

But Dumphee didn't believe that could happen. Most folks said the earth was far older than six thousand years. If they were right, then Dumphee figured he'd likely get himself in real trouble if he tried bumping that machine again. Who knew what would happen? He might end up fighting Martians in the future. Or what if he went way back in time, before the earth had a breathable atmosphere? What if he found himself on Earth when it was all a bunch of hot lava rock?

No, it would be dangerous to play with that time machine. Meanwhile, he had some weapons—weapons he didn't know how to use.

He glanced up at Lotsa Smoke, who was carving into the buffalo, blood up to her elbows. Firelight flickered on the animal's fur. Something seemed wrong. She must have sensed that he was watching her. She glanced up and smiled, holding the knife in her right hand and a strip of meat in the other.

"Why are you cutting so much?" Dumphee asked, suddenly realizing that the squaws planned to dry the whole buffalo.

Lotsa Smoke waved toward a recently finished smoking rack, where she'd already hung twenty pounds of meat. A smudge fire burned beneath it. "No can always get good dog to eat."

―ттｎ｡ꞇ―

That night, stripped buffalo bones lay beside the crackling fires. In the firelight, the squaws lay all around. Bear Tail staked the buffalo hide to the ground, and slept atop it, while Pretty Rose covered herself with leaves. She belched pleasantly in her stupor. Lotsa Smoke curled up in the grass by the truck.

Dumphee sat with his back against a wheel of the ATV, wondering at the strangeness of the scene. He was pleasantly full of meat. The buffalo hadn't tasted anything like beef. It was gamy and tough. Still, it filled his belly.

In the woods, he heard the distant hoot of an owl, and the familiar snarl of a bobcat. Far away, wolves barked—a sound he'd never heard in West Virginia.

He began to wonder about that. He'd always loved animals, and began thinking about all the animals that had gone extinct in the past couple hundred years: the dodo bird, the passenger pigeon, the Tasmanian devil. He wondered if he could go around collecting all these animals, then maybe kick the time machine until he got back into the future. Maybe he could rescue whole species of animals somehow, become sort of a modern-day Noah.

The idea appealed to him, yet he thought it would be a lonely task. He felt out of his element. He got a couple of army blankets from the truck and threw them on the ground, then lay between them like a piece of ham between two slices of rye.

He'd hardly laid down, when Lotsa Smoke crept up and nuzzled in beside him.

He glanced at her over his shoulder. In the firelight her eyes shone expectantly.

In horror, Dumphee leapt from under the blankets and climbed up a tire of the ATV, onto its fender and hood. Lotsa Smoke smiled as if it were a game and made a grab for him. Dumphee scurried up over the cab of the ATV and onto the canvas top.

Lotsa Smoke tried to get a grip on the hood of the truck and climb after him. Then she stood, her smile faltering, and stared.

"What wrong?" she asked, the words catching in her throat. "What matter with you?"

"Stay down there!" Dumphee said.

Lotsa Smoke slid back down to the ground, crestfallen. Tears began to water her eyes. Then she puffed out her chest in defiance and stood like some great chief. She thumped her breast with her hand. "Me great squaw! Missionaries like Lotsa Smoke. Seneca like Lotsa Smoke. You like Lotsa Smoke, too. You see!"

Dumphee sat on the canvas, shaking his head, unable to speak. He'd never thought himself prudish, but—he felt it would be wrong to make love to her this way. He was her owner. Her slave master.

Or maybe he wasn't, he realized. Indian men bought and sold squaws, yet both parties considered the women to be wives. Was a wife only a slave? Or was she something more? Maybe he didn't really understand the relationship that had formed between them.

"What?" Lotsa Smoke said. "You no like me? You want other squaw?"

"No—no, not that!" Dumphee said. "Look, Lotsa Smoke, it ain't nothin' personal, see. You're a fine-looking woman. God knows you're a fine-looking woman. But—I don't want any slaves. I couldn't treat a woman like that. And a fellow can't just go around with three wives. That's uncivilized!"

With that accusation, it was as if he'd slapped her face. He suddenly understood where she'd got her name. He never saw a woman get so angry so fast. Lotsa Smoke made a low growling noise. "Civilize? Civilize? I no civilize enough for you?"

From the tears that glistened in her eyes, it looked as if the accusation nearly destroyed her. She silently reached for her knife in its sheath. Fortunately, she'd laid her blade aside a few moments ago. Lotsa Smoke sneered. "You want some French missy? I know how she dress! I smell . . ." She searched for a word, spoke with a French accent, *"parfum!"*

"No—it's not that!" Dumphee said, wishing he could take his words back. "I don't want any other women."

But Lotsa Smoke suddenly gave a blood-curdling cry and began shouting at the other women in Mohawk. Pretty Rose and Bear Tail both leapt up and rushed toward the truck as if to discover the cause of the commotion. They listened to Lotsa Smoke yammering in Mohawk for a moment, then they, too, began shouting at Dumphee.

"What did you tell them?" Dumphee yelled at Lotsa Smoke.

"I tell them you say they no good squaws!" she answered.

Dumphee dodged a rock that Pretty Rose hurled, while Bear Tail hunted for a long stick to club him with. A big rock bounced off Dumphee's head as Lotsa Smoke blindsided him. He dropped to the canvas atop the rig and covered himself, began rolling right and left to escape the hail of stones and sticks that assailed him.

"Stop! Please, stop! I give up!" Dumphee said.

As one, the three women all stared up at him, scowling.

Bear Tail growled, "Are squaws good?"

"Yes, yes," Dumphee wailed.

"Better than perfect?" Pretty Rose asked.

"Of course. All good. You're all very fine, beautiful, precious young women. I respect you and admire you as my equals."

"Good!" Lotsa Smoke said, the quarrel settled.

———

Pretty Rose and Lotsa Smoke lay beside Dumphee, naked, curled beneath each of his arms.

Dumphee thought of Jo Beth, back home. He wondered if he'd ever find her again, wondered if he should go take a look at that time machine and try to figure out how to get back to

West Virginia. But, somehow, he suspected that he was stuck here in the past, and ought to make the best of it.

At the foot of his bed, Bear Tail wriggled out from under her buckskin dress to stand fully naked in the light of the campfire, her eyes wide and wanton.

She nodded slowly, as if reading his mind, then licked her lips. "Me show you Mohawk way," she whispered seductively.

In his left ear, Pretty Rose whispered, "And after Bear Tail finish, me show you Mingo way." She nuzzled him and licked his ear.

On his right, Lotsa Smoke kissed his jaw, and her hand reached down and stroked his bare skin, sliding along his belly. "And . . . oh . . . when they finish, me show you . . . oh . . . Quaker way. You like!"

Lotsa Smoke shot Pretty Rose and Bear Tail a warning glance. "Don't wear brave out."

As Bear Tail opened the blankets and began crawling up between his legs, Dumphee lay with heart pounding. Three women at once? Here he was, sleeping with three beautiful women at once. He wondered if maybe civilization hadn't been overrated.

CHAPTER 10

At dawn, just before the sun rose in a ball of wild pink, soft clouds of mist began to rise from the river. The squaws woke early and began packing buffalo meat and hides into the back of the truck.

Dumphee did not help, merely watched from the cab. He flipped on his Walkman, hoping the time machine might have spirited him back to his time, hoping that perhaps it had some automatic homing device.

But only the now familiar static issued from the radio.

After several long minutes, Dumphee screwed up his courage and went to the back of the truck. He took out a Russian commando knife and carefully began to unpack the time machine. He worried the blade under each nail, popped it free, and then pulled off the top of the crate.

A pulsing blue light shone from the cracks under the lid even as he set the top aside.

What he saw baffled him. Inside the crate, two posts of blackened metal protruded from a black base. The posts were each perhaps a foot tall, and were set about thirty-six inches apart.

Between those posts lay a chamber of glass. Each pane looked very thick, perhaps four inches. Inside that glass, a blue light throbbed, dancing wildly.

Dumphee had no idea what the light was, yet on each blackened post, computer screens showed readings in red. Dumphee stared at the Cyrillic letters, trying to decipher a word or two. There were no dates written in red, at least not that he could tell. He'd hoped for some kind of sliding scale, with dates below it, and an arrow that he could adjust by hand to the year 1991.

But one look at these complex computer screens convinced him that this was some kind of government project. Maybe even Einstein wouldn't have been able to figure the whole thing out.

For the longest time, Dumphee was tempted to bang on the machine, to see what would happen.

He worried. He had his duty to consider. He was charged with taking this equipment to Denver; he wondered if he ought to head west, on the off chance that the machine did have some sort of auto relay.

If the machine returned him to the future, would it send him back to the exact moment he'd left, or would it let time pass naturally? In other words, would each day that he spent here equal a day of time in the future?

He supposed that Lieutenant Fugg *might* help decode the screens. Maybe he could read Russian. But Dumphee rejected that notion. Fugg wasn't the kind of fellow who would learn Russian, unless he could learn it in his sleep.

There have to be Russians alive today—Dumphee reasoned—someone who might tell me what the red characters mean.

I know what they say, Dumphee told himself as he studied the script. They say you shouldn't ought to have bumped this danged machine in the first place.

Hadn't some Russians settled in Alaska, originally? Dumphee remembered that from his fourth-grade history class. And if Russians had settled in Alaska, he might find some there now, and maybe they could read the computer screens for him. But he'd have to drive across country to reach them.

Dumphee placed the lid back on the box and considered his options. No matter what he did—whether he stayed here or drove on—he'd need some clothes, matches and decent food. So the first thing he had to do was get supplies. Foremost among those supplies, he needed fuel. Gasoline wasn't in use in this time zone, he knew. But other things were: coal oil, maybe, or whale blubber.

Or alcohol.

There had been a trading post back at Fort Pitt. But he couldn't go back to it.

Dumphee surveyed the contents of the truck: buffalo meat, a few army rations, the commando knives, several sealed crates and a time machine. He cracked open the sealed boxes and found dozens of futuristic-looking grenades, a Russian hand-held antiaircraft gun and ten strange rifles with long, almost needle-thin barrels.

He began to repack the weapons, to keep from jostling the time machine, when outside the truck he heard shouts and whooping.

Bear Tail raced past the back of the truck, two warriors chasing her.

A fierce-looking warrior with a hat of red porcupine quills and a face painted white with blue spots suddenly rounded the back of the truck, looked in at Dumphee, eyes wide. He had a war lance in one hand, a hide shield in the other.

The warrior hurled his lance.

Dumphee ducked as the lance whipped past his face. Without thinking, Dumphee grabbed the nearest weapon— the antiaircraft gun. He thumbed a red arming switch on the handle of the gun, and shouted, "You gonna die, boy!"

The warrior must have seen death in Dumphee's eyes, or perhaps he feared the strange weapon, for he screamed, backed from the truck and broke into a run.

Dumphee leapt out into the open. Over by the drying racks, four warriors struggled over Lotsa Smoke and Pretty Rose. The Indian maidens kicked and scratched like wildcats. Some petty chief raised a tomahawk, preparing to scalp Lotsa Smoke.

"My tomahawk is bigger than yours!" Dumphee shouted. He pointed the antiaircraft gun and squeezed the trigger.

The chief looked up at Dumphee, and his jaw dropped.

With a roar the missile disengaged from the launcher and burst forward.

It must have been a heat-seeking missile, for it veered toward the fire, whipped between two warriors, slammed into the meat-drying racks and carried them away. The missile hit an alder tree fifty yards outside camp and exploded in a fireball that rose some three hundred feet in the air.

The chief—a distinguished-looking fellow with red stripes painted down his face—wet his breechcloth and fainted.

The rest of the warriors raced into the brush quicker than hares running from a hound.

"Come back and fight!" Pretty Rose screamed at the retreating warriors as she finally freed her knife.

Lotsa Smoke got up from the ground, staring at Dumphee with awe in her eyes. Suddenly she recognized that he was more than your average paleface. "Where you come from? What you do? You great war chief?"

"No," Dumphee said. "I just helped my pappy make the best moonshine in Upshaw County."

"Uh," she said thoughtfully. "Big medicine man. You make sunshine too?"

Dumphee would have explained what he did right then, but Pretty Rose, who had put her knife away, now picked up a long stick and began beating the unconscious chief.

Bear Tail ran back into camp and kicked the man.

He roused a bit and lashed out with a foot in self-defense, but Lotsa Smoke whipped out her commando knife and pressed the edge to his throat.

"Hey, now," Dumphee said, not liking the anger in the squaws' eyes. "What are you going to do with him?"

"Him we gonna torture. We put sticks in skin, set on fire. Then take scalp and kill."

"But—you can't do that!" Dumphee said. "What about respect for your fellow Native Americans? What about human rights?"

"He no respect us if we no torture," Lotsa Smoke said. "He just come back with more braves."

"But—" Dumphee began to say.

"He our prisoner!" Lotsa Smoke objected, and the look of hatred in her eye was so intense, Dumphee took a step back. "Manitou be angry if we no kill him."

"All right, all right," Dumphee conceded, suddenly recalling something about Indian torture techniques. "How long is this all going to take?"

"Two days," Bear Tail said with a wicked giggle. "Maybe three."

"Three days? Three whole days?" Dumphee shouted. "I don't think so. I'm on a schedule. I'm supposed to have that vehicle full of vital military equipment in Denver in two days. That means we have to leave *now!*"

"No have time for torture?" Lotsa Smoke asked.

"Right," Dumphee said. "And as my pappy used to say, 'If you can't do a job right, you might as well not do it at all.'"

"So you let our prisoner go, and start helping me figure out where I can get some firewater."

"Firewater?" all three squaws asked at once, turning to Dumphee, the prisoner nearly forgotten.

"That's right," Dumphee said. "I need a heap lot of fire-water."

"Frenchmen have heap firewater. They trade to Seneca for English scalps."

The very thought made Dumphee queasy. "Remind me to punch the next Canadian I see," he grumbled. "Then, it sounds like we'd be doing the English a favor if we appropriate some firewater."

Dumphee went to the fearsome-looking chief. Lotsa Smoke still had her knife to his throat. The fellow was at least a foot shorter than Dumphee, and the way Dumphee had been shouting, the chief seemed terrified.

Dumphee said to Lotsa Smoke, "You tell him that we want him to lead us to the Frenchman's firewater."

"No need him. I know where go get firewater," Lotsa Smoke retorted.

"Tell him anyway," Dumphee said. "I'm the chief around here."

Lotsa Smoke spat a few words in French, liberally interspersed with curses.

The Seneca cursed back.

"What did he say?" Dumphee asked.

"He big brave, no gonna talk," Lotsa Smoke answered. "He say lots bad things about your mother. She English pig who sleep with dog. He hope you kill him fast, now. Not want to get torture."

"I know," Pretty Rose said with a wicked grin. "Let's take him with us. We have fun cutting off little pieces; feed him to coyotes.

Dumphee gently took the knife from Lotsa Smoke, keeping it against the warrior's throat. "All right, you women get in the ATV. I'll take care of this guy."

Lotsa Smoke's eyes shone with excitement. "We watch!"

"No, you get in the truck. I'll handle him!" Dumphee shouted.

Reluctantly, the squaws complied. The little chief gazed fiercely at Dumphee.

Dumphee said, "So, you scalp my people and insult my parentage? Well, so much for multiculturalism and ethnic diversity, you little 'coon turd!"

The warrior began breathing curses against Dumphee in mixed French and English and Seneca. Dumphee studied the fellow. He'd planned to let him go, but now saw such bitterness in the man's face, such seething hatred, he knew that to do so would be a mistake. This fellow would likely go on killing and butchering white settlers.

Yet Dumphee couldn't just kill a man.

Dumphee didn't know what to do.

When the women got in the vehicle, Dumphee kept the knife against the Seneca's throat for a moment, then eased up from his crouch and slowly backed to the truck.

The Seneca warrior stood and walked toward him, chest thrust out. He paced stiff-legged toward Dumphee, hurling insults at the top of his lungs.

Dumphee got in the truck and started it, with a low growl. In the cab, Lotsa Smoke and Pretty Rose both sat stiffly, fists clenched, so angry that tears watered their eyes.

They were ashamed of him, he could tell, ashamed that he was so soft, that he'd let an enemy go.

The Seneca stood in front of the truck, hurling invectives. Dumphee stared as the little man began pounding the hood of the truck. Dumphee had always thought his white ancestors must have been monsters to have treated the Indians so badly, to have killed them and taken their land.

Now he wasn't so sure. Here was a man whose code of honor demanded that he fight. Here was a warrior who would kill Dumphee and the squaws without a thought. Who wouldn't hesitate to torture them, or to take Dumphee's squaws as sex slaves. Here was a fellow who wouldn't reason or *simply walk away.*

This Seneca and the squaws weren't uncivilized, either, Dumphee knew. But they lived by different rules. Rules that made their culture and his incompatible.

The Seneca shouted a particularly vile profanity in English, and slammed both hands on the hood of the ATV.

"Well, to hell with you, too, buddy!" Dumphee shouted, and then he punched the horn so hard that his palm hurt.

The air horn belched loud, and the chief leapt in terror so high that Dumphee wondered if the man had just set a world record for the highest leap from a standing position. The chief turned to run.

Dumphee shifted the truck into gear and chased after him. All three squaws began shouting and squealing in delight at this new game.

Dumphee pressed the *Armaments* button, and the machine gun sprouted up from the hood.

The warrior raced over open ground, heading alongside the muddy riverbed, leaping driftwood. Dumphee followed on his tail, blasting his horn again and again.

Each time he did so, the warrior glanced back and grimaced in terror. Dumphee timed one blast just so, and the warrior stubbed his toe on a log and rolled into the mud.

A toggle let Dumphee aim the machine gun; he aimed below the war chief's feet and began firing.

The warrior flung himself aside, crawled splashing into the shallows of the river, and dodged as Dumphee pretended he would run him over.

Dumphee spun a U-turn, whipped around after the Seneca, blasted his horn again.

The fellow leapt into deep water, perhaps hoping it would save him, and Dumphee hit the accelerator, set his tires spinning through the waves.

The chief was swimming with long strokes when the right-front ATV tire hit him, shoving him underwater.

The squaws squealed in triumph. Lotsa Smoke thumped her fists against the dashboard, though Dumphee knew the water was so deep that running over the warrior wouldn't do much more than put the fear of God into him. He'd only get shoved under for a couple of seconds.

Sure enough, when Dumphee looked in his rearview mirror, he saw the Seneca come up sputtering for air. Dumphee figured that it was over, that he'd scared the fellow straight. But it didn't satisfy Bear Tail, who sat in the back of the truck.

She grabbed an M-16 and raced to the tailgate. Dumphee was sure she didn't know how to work the gun, but quick as lightning she released the safety and squeezed off half a clip, bullets stinging the water around the Seneca warrior.

The fellow swallowed some air, dove quickly, and Dumphee saw from his bare butt that he had lost his breechcloth.

"I think you finished him," Dumphee called to Bear Tail. "Good job!"

There was a look of genuine relief in Bear Tail's face, and Dumphee wondered what horrors these women had suffered at the hands of the Seneca. "He dead?" she asked.

"Yeah, he's dead," Dumphee lied. He was certain the Seneca was merely underwater, holding his breath.

Lotsa Smoke turned to him with a greedy look, "Go back and get scalp!"

"We don't have time," Dumphee said. He hit the gas, hurrying downriver, around a bend.

CHAPTER 11

In Denver, Major Slice stood in his office, gazing over his reports. The captain who'd brought the reports, an impeccably military fellow named Smith, was a security specialist —the kind who truly only revealed information on a need-to-know basis.

"Give it all to me straight, Captain," Slice said, nervously batting his swagger stick against the side of his shoe. He inhaled a deep breath from his cigar.

"As our reports say, the ATV bearing the time machine has come up missing. The transmitter on the vehicle ceased sending its signal at precisely 1:14 last night. Our global positioning satellites have confirmed the location of the truck where it exited our time line.

"A search of its intended route shows that gasoline was purchased by our men at 1:04 a.m., just outside Pittsburgh. So we know that the truck was in our possession then. A few minutes later, the vehicle was spotted eight miles farther on, and nearly crashed into a fast-food restaurant.

"Witnesses say that a large, strangely shaped vehicle—one witness described it as a spaceship—was hurtling toward the McDonald's at a hundred miles per hour when it vanished in a peach-colored light."

"Peach colored?" Major Slice said. "You sure it wasn't more of a rufous hue, perhaps even fawn or cochineal?"

"Uh, witnesses called it 'peach,' sir. Though one woman called it ecru."

"Ecru? Ecru? I'll be damned," Slice said.

"Yes, sir," the captain agreed.

"Well, what else have you found?" Slice demanded.

"We did a quick check of the historical archives of the University of Pennsylvania, and found that a number of time-anomalous items turned up from an excavation near Fort Pitt in 1939. All of them were found in a single coffin, and were sent to Washington, D.C., as is standard procedure in such cases."

"Do we get a lot of these time-anomalous items?" Slice asked.

"I could tell you, sir," the security officer said, "but you know the standard reply." His voice suddenly took on a note of glee, "I can promise to make your death quick and painless though, if you're curious enough."

Just once, Major Slice was tempted to ask the question anyway, just to find out how many "time-anomalous" ray guns had turned up, or how many extraterrestrials the government had pickled in brine.

Sure, they'd kill him afterward. But, then, no one lives forever.

"So what did we find?"

"These," Captain Smith answered. He handed over a corroded pair of dog tags, some coins, half a rusted Timex. The dog tags were Fugg's.

"What do you make of it?" Major Slice asked.

"Well, the ATV had plenty of gas, so it's apparent that Private Dumphee remained at the wheel. What happened to him, we may never know. We don't have any vehicle remains fitting this description among our time-anomalous artifacts."

"I see . . ." Major Slice said. "What can you tell me about this Dumphee?"

"He's a buck private from West Virginia who enlisted under duress."

"Economic duress? Or was he trying to escape a pregnant girlfriend?"

"No, sir. Judicial duress. He was convicted of moonshining and given a choice between enlistment and prison."

"A moonshiner?" Slice groused. "That explains the erratic driving. I'll bet he's all liquored up. Damn him. Heads are going to roll over this! Tell me, what are the chances that he'll get back to present day?"

"From what I can tell," Smith said, "the machine wasn't precalibrated."

"Which means what, precisely?"

"The chances are . . . almost nonexistent."

"Well then," Major Slice said, "we'll just have to court-martial the son of a bitch in absentia!"

CHAPTER 12

Somehow his attack against the French lacked the emotional intensity Dumphee would have expected. He'd thought he'd have to go to some huge fort, knock a hole through a wall with an antiaircraft gun, shoot the place up a bit, then find the whiskey or whatever the hell it was that men drank.

Nothin' doing. Instead, the ATV lazily drifted down the Ohio River most of the afternoon, idling, catching the sunlight. A pair of otters swam beside the truck for a long way, and Dumphee watched the huge trout in the deeper pools, wishing once again that he had his fishing rod.

The squaws sat in back of the truck, singing Christian hymns that Dumphee had mostly never heard. One of them found Lieutenant Fugg's sunglasses, and for an hour the squaws took turns looking through them. Pretty Rose wanted to keep them all for herself, for she said they made her look "more like a bug."

Dumphee got out his little Walkman, fished through his duffel bag until he found his tapes, put in Flatt & Scruggs, then gave Lotsa Smoke a listen.

Her eyes grew wide, and she stared at Dumphee in awe.

"How you put little man in there?" Lotsa Smoke demanded.

Dumphee grinned slyly. "I didn't. It's just his spirit. And you girls better be good and do what I tell you, or I'll put your spirits in there, too."

Almost immediately he regretted the joke, for Lotsa Smoke leaned away from him, abject terror on her face, while Pretty Rose grabbed for the headphones.

Lotsa Smoke pushed the Walkman away, as if glad to get rid of it, and Pretty Rose listened for a long time. By the time Flatt & Scruggs had gotten through "Pain in My Heart," Pretty Rose was crying. "Maybe you *should* put squaw's soul in there," she said. "Little man sound heap lonely."

"Hmmm...." Dumphee said, astonished at her generosity. He drove the truck onto the beach, roared beside the river, scattering herds of buffalo.

Once he passed a Seneca village where fields of corn were planted beside the long houses. He honked his horn and sent the villagers running.

Near dusk he reached the French trading post by the river, a log hut where a couple of bateaux lay dragged up half out of the water.

Outside the trading post, beaver and otter hides lay in a dirty heap. Bear and beaver traps hung along the wall. Smoke curled from the chimney, and two old Senecas squatted by the door. A crude sign above them said *Pierre et Pierre, Commerçant.*

When they saw the ATV roll out of the water, the Senecas ran into the building, shouting.

Dumphee knew there would be trouble. He leaned back thoughtfully and told the squaws, "*Pierre et Pierre,* eh? Ladies, it's time to party." He pressed the *Armaments* button on his console, let the fifty-caliber machine gun hover into view.

A pair of fat, bearded Frenchmen came running from the trading post, loading their flintlocks. Both men wore buckskins. One wore a coonskin hat, while the other wore a red Phrygian stocking cap. The Senecas rushed out behind them.

While the Frenchmen loaded their guns, Dumphee drove within ten feet of the door and honked his horn. One fellow dropped his gun and backed against the wall, hands raised. The other nervously spilled powder from his horn, but kept trying to load his weapon.

Dumphee opened his door and asked, "Hey, Pierre? You speak English?"

"*Oui,*" the fellow under the coonskin said, face pale.

"Then throw down your damned gun," Dumphee said. He toggled the controls for the ATV's fifty-caliber and sprayed bullets above the men's heads.

Both men dropped to their knees and raised their hands. One began praying loudly.

"Get in your boats and get out of here," Dumphee added for good measure.

The Frenchmen and Senecas rushed for the bateaux, shoved them into the water and rowed away.

For a moment, Dumphee stood outside the trading post, wondering if the squaws had been wrong about these two. This didn't look like any French military outpost engaged in nefarious deals, trading firewater for English scalps.

Inside the hut, Dumphee found things pretty much as one might expect. The store was packed to the ceiling with candles and glass lamps and bottles of whale oil; musket balls, hatchets, knives and cooking pots; trapping supplies; matches and turpentine, cloth, thread; dried beans and salt.

The squaws began pulling needles and beads from the shelves. Bear Tail took all four mirrors, along with a little telescope.

Dumphee looked around, then went into a back room. He found kegs of gunpowder stacked against a wall, and several twenty-five-gallon barrels of whiskey.

Dangling from the rafters were human scalps.

Dumphee glanced at one scrap of red hair, and whispered, "Well, Mr. Macdonald—it is nice to meet the rest of you."

But even this grim jest could not shield him from a creeping sense of horror. There were other scalps—the blonde scalp of a little girl, with blue bows in the hair; the fawn-colored ponytail of a woman.

Dumphee gaped at them for a long moment, horror and revulsion rising from within. He remembered one of his sociology teachers in high school reading from an article written in a national magazine at the turn of the twentieth century. The article talked about the wonderful improvements in "interracial relations" at the time. Apparently, back then, interracial relations meant the relations between the English and the French, for the article spoke about the wonderful new friendship developing between the countries.

Here, now, Dumphee finally understood why folks had once thought the French inhuman. Had he seen these scalps hanging outside the trading post, he'd have shot *Mssrs. Pierre et Pierre* where they stood.

Sickened, Dumphee decided he needed a drink. He tapped a keg and drank from a tin cup.

"Hmmm . . . 130 proof," he guessed, then he breathed it in and out over his tongue, and raised his estimate. "More like 140, or 142."

It wasn't the best-tasting liquor he'd ever drunk, but he supposed it would run a truck.

"Let's load up, squaws," he shouted. Somehow, that didn't sound respectful. After a bit of thought, he corrected himself, "*Wives.* Let's load, *wives.*"

The women were stealing everything in the trading post: bolts of cloth, rounds of cheese, kegs of salt. He drew the line when they started pulling down the leg traps. "Not those, Bear Tail," he grumbled. "Where I come from, we only wear synthetic furs."

Bear Tail studied him a moment, a puzzled expression on her face. "Will you catch-em a synthetic for me? I skin it and tan it."

"Sure," Dumphee said. "I'll shoot the first one I see."

For the next half-hour, they looted the trading post. When Dumphee left, he burned the place to the ground.

—⊓⊓⊤⊓⊓—

Dumphee sat behind the wheel of the ATV, crawling over the plains west of Pittsburgh in the early evening, sometimes gently dropping into buffalo wallows, then rising again into the night. Bats flitted around the vehicle, snapping up insects that jumped into the air as the ATV passed.

To the south, Dumphee spotted the smoke from cooking fires in an Indian village. Lotsa Smoke took Dumphee's shirt and began sewing beads around his nametag.

Dumphee found himself dreaming of Coca-Cola. He glanced into the bed of the truck. Bear Tail sat on a keg of gunpowder, cradling a machine gun, gazing at the trail behind.

"We stop now, set camp," Lotsa Smoke said to Dumphee. "It dark outside."

"No, we'll keep on going." He'd decided to strike out for Denver, whether he could ever make it or not.

He flipped on the headlights, and Lotsa Smoke gasped at the miraculous light. In the brush to their left, a huge bull moose, its antlers still in velvet, rushed for deeper cover.

"I need to rest my eyes," Dumphee said. "You think you could drive for a while?"

Lotsa Smoke gulped.

"It's easy," Dumphee said. "If you want to go faster, just push the gas, like this. And if you want to stop, push the brakes. The gearshift is automatic. There's no clutch."

Lotsa Smoke gulped again as he demonstrated how to drive. After a few minutes, he managed to coax her behind the wheel. "Just make sure you don't go over any big bumps," Dumphee said. "And wake me if you have questions."

"Ugh," Lotsa Smoke grunted. She took the wheel solemnly and began driving with great care, almost afraid to steer. Dumphee watched her for half an hour, then closed his eyes.

An hour later Dumphee lay snoring as Lotsa Smoke drove. She had no idea where she was going, but dared not wake Dumphee to tell him, for fear that he'd never let her drive the A-teepee again.

Instead, she pressed the gas more firmly and sped over the grasslands, through brush and reeds that almost reached the top of the hood.

Dumphee and Pretty Rose were asleep, Pretty Rose leaning against the door, Dumphee lying with his head against her shoulder.

Bear Tail climbed to the little window between the cab and the back of the vehicle, humming "Rock of Ages." She giggled into Lotsa Smoke's ear. Her breath smelled strongly of fire-water.

"You thirsty?" Bear Tail asked in Mohawk. She pushed a tin cup into Lotsa Smoke's hand.

Lotsa Smoke took one swallow. It burned her throat, so she drank the whole cup quickly.

Bear Tail laughed and refilled the cup. "What we get all firewater for, if not for drink?"

"Chief say we get firewater to feed to A-teepee on wheels," Lotsa Smoke answered.

"If A-teepee drink all firewater," Bear Tail said, "it will not walk straight."

"Ugh," Lotsa Smoke nodded agreement, for Bear Tail sounded wise beyond her years.

"Maybe we should drink firewater, and fill kegs with river water," Bear Tail suggested.

"Good idea," Lotsa Smoke said.

She finished drinking another cup of firewater, and found it hard to keep her eyes open. The moving A-teepee swerved erratically. She steered hard right and left a few times, testing it more than she'd dared.

Dumphee's snoring caught. He half raised his head, then went back to sleep.

Bear Tail began giggling in the back of the truck again. She crawled a pace for some more firewater and fell down helplessly.

Lotsa Smoke hit the accelerator and sped over the fields.

The lights shone on a wolf, and Lotsa Smoke veered toward it. The wolf began racing over the prairie. Lotsa Smoke pressed the gas harder, just as Bear Tail came back to the window, giggling.

Bear Tail pointed across the prairie. "No get wolf. Get buffalo!"

There Lotsa Smoke saw the dark humps of a huge herd of buffalo out in the fields. They were sleeping.

She giggled and spun the wheel, heading toward the buffalo herd. The headlights played on dark shapes, and suddenly Lotsa Smoke was racing through the herd, the buffaloes rushing pell-mell to escape—calves and cows and even old bulls.

She pounded the horn as Dumphee had done, and spun the wheel, circling back around after one big bull.

At the sound of the horn, the bull turned and charged the vehicle, its great shaggy head slamming into the front fender.

The whole truck jolted, and Lotsa Smoke found herself thrown against the steering wheel.

A beautiful glow filled the air, like clouds at sunrise.

"What the hell?" Dumphee shouted, rousing from his sleep to stare, terrified, out the window.

"Ah, pretty!" Bear Tail cried in wonder at the sight.

Then the ATV was gliding over icy windblown fields in the blinding daylight. A huge wall of fractured ice reared up before them, some hundred feet high.

The squaws all screamed and threw up their hands as the ATV plowed toward it.

Dumphee shouted in terror and slammed the brake with his left foot.

The truck slue sideways as Lotsa Smoke turned the wheel, then skidded to a halt mere inches from the ice wall.

Lotsa Smoke squinted in her drunken stupor and held her head up. "Oh! Winter come fast this year!"

CHAPTER 13

Dumphee flipped on the radio of his Sony Walkman.

Still no reassuring music.

And the huge wall of ice didn't look like anything that could have formed during a normal storm—or even a long winter.

The river was gone, as well as the warm plains with their herds of buffalo. Dumphee smelled firewater. "All right," Dumphee growled at Lotsa Smoke, "what happened?"

Lotsa Smoke wrapped her arms around herself to keep out the cold. She stared blankly at the ice. "Winter come very fast," she groaned. "Much snow. Was terrible storm. Hit something in storm."

"Oh, no you don't," Dumphee said. "You've been drinking firewater! You got drunk, and you ran into something!"

"Manitou mad at us!" Lotsa Smoke said. "He do this!"

"Don't blame it on Manitou," Dumphee said. "You know better than that! You're Christians."

"No can be too sure," Pretty Rose said in Lotsa Smoke's defense. "When Christian God get mad, he send sinners to hell. Is very hot. Hotter than this. This Manitou's work."

Lotsa Smoke turned on Dumphee, her jaw clenched, chin raised, and said with fire in her eyes, "Manitou angry because you no let us torture Seneca. It *your* fault."

"Don't blame it on me, either," Dumphee warned. "You're drunk. You've been into the firewater. What did you hit?"

"Manitou come in shape of sacred white buffalo. It run at us, hit A-teepee on wheels."

"A buffalo," Dumphee repeated, gritting his teeth. Lotsa Smoke wore a belligerent, guilty look. He wondered.

Maybe it really wasn't her fault. Dumphee didn't know much about buffaloes, and one could never tell what a wild animal would do, especially one that had never seen a truck.

Even if it was Lotsa Smoke's fault, there was nothing for it.

Dumphee climbed over Lotsa Smoke and went out to inspect the damage. Surprisingly, the front of the truck didn't look too bad. The ATV had a bumper made from a wide strip of metal, covered over with some thick plastic. There was a little scuffed paint, a bit of horn embedded in the bumper. Otherwise, it looked fine. Fortunately, the buffalo hadn't rammed a headlight.

He hurried back into the cab of the ATV, out of the cold. It wasn't really bitterly cold outside—maybe only twenty-five degrees—but a strong wind blew over the ice, so that the wind chill made it feel worse. Bear Tail began rummaging in the back of the vehicle, pulling out blankets, laying down the uncured buffalo hide to keep her warm. The other women huddled together, looking miserably cold. Dumphee didn't have any warm clothes himself, aside from an army jacket in his duffel bag.

He pulled out the army jacket, tossed it back to Bear Tail, then cranked up the heat in the cab. As hot air began seeping through the vents, Lotsa Smoke and Pretty Rose greedily put their hands over the grill.

"Ladies, we are in heap big trouble," Dumphee told them. "And we are in heap big trouble together. We are stuck in the far past. You know what the past is?"

"Many moons ago?" Pretty Rose asked, looking up from the grill. "Before Columbus?"

Lotsa Smoke shot Dumphee an angry look, as if she suspected he was lying.

"That's right: many, many, many moons ago. I don't know how many for sure, but I've got a bad feeling about this. So here is what we're going to do. We're going to have to keep this *A-tee-vee* running so that it will keep the engine warm for as long as we can. That way, the heat will keep coming out of these vents. Understand?"

"Good idea—keep Injun warm," Pretty Rose agreed.

"Where fire?" Lotsa Smoke asked suspiciously, not taking her hand from the vent.

"We have a fire inside the engine, which makes the truck go. That's how the ATV runs. The engine needs firewater to run."

"Where smoke from fire?" Lotsa Smoke asked, still skeptical.

"It's coming out the tailpipe of the truck. The smoke hole—" he pointed into the rearview mirror on the passenger side and showed her the smoke coming out.

When she saw it, Lotsa Smoke grinned in relief, as if she had feared some kind of deception.

"I wouldn't lie to you," Dumphee told her. To his surprise, Lotsa Smoke leaned over and cuddled against his shoulder.

"You say magic teepee travel in time, like wagon travel on ground?" Pretty Rose asked.

"That's right," Dumphee said. "When Lotsa Smoke hit that buffalo, we traveled far back in time."

"Then maybe—for me—you take teepee to day when Seneca kill mother, and we shoot bad Seneca? Make bad thing never happen."

Dumphee looked into Pretty Rose's eyes, saw calculation and pleading and real pain there. She understood. He'd thought that maybe, since she was a savage, she wouldn't have been able to grasp what had happened. But she understood the time machine as well as he did. We're both savages together, he realized.

"If I knew how, Pretty Rose, I would. But I don't know how to do that. You see, there is a machine in the bed of the truck."

He turned and pointed at the box. "And we're not supposed to bump it. When we do, then the truck travels through time. But I don't know how to control it—how to make us go to the right time. So far, this machine has only taken me backward in time. Your mother hasn't been born yet. I don't know if this vehicle even *can* move us forward through time."

Pretty Rose absorbed his words thoughtfully. "I see," she said at last. "You come from time after us, then."

"That's right, I came from your future. Many, many moons in your future. I came from 1991, hundreds of years from when you were born."

"That why have teepee that move on ground without help of horse or ox, and have heap big rifle."

"That's right."

Lotsa Smoke frowned in thought. "Then English will win war? Kill French and Seneca?"

Dumphee was impressed by the squaw's deduction. "Yes, all Seneca dead, and many French."

"Mohawks live though. Yes?"

The answer caught in Dumphee's throat, "Yes."

Lotsa Smoke studied him a moment, then smiled in relief.

Dumphee looked up at the map shining on the inside of the windshield. A musket ball had put a small hole near the spot, but Dumphee could still see half of the map. "We'll head south," he said, torn between the desire to angle toward Denver and the need to get to warmer climes. He dropped the ATV into gear, and headed over the frozen ice.

CHAPTER 14

The ATV made poor time on the ice. Too many ruptures and cracks in the frozen ground made the going uneven. He figured that it must be spring, for the ice was melting, and once the vehicle dropped beneath him as the ATV broke through a thin crust of ice and found itself floating in a raging torrent. A river had carved a path under the ice, hidden by a layer of snow.

Dumphee was able to get the vehicle to climb out of the water—but only barely. No human or animal that had the misfortune of traversing that spot would ever have made it alive from the frigid water.

Dumphee wheeled over eighty miles of ice and snow in eight hours. By the middle of the night he found he was too tired to go on.

He gave the wheel back to Lotsa Smoke, who had sobered, and showed her how to navigate using the map that projected onto the windshield. According to the map, they were outside Wheeling, West Virginia. He could see the snow-covered mountains of home in the distance.

After a long while, he slept.

He woke to the sound of the horn blaring. It was dawn, and the ATV had come off the ice and was rolling through a forest of jack pine. The temperature had warmed dramatically, and Lotsa Smoke wound through the pines, honking the horn at a herd of musk oxen that snorted and darted away.

"We come to big town, I think," Lotsa Smoke told Dumphee triumphantly. "I drive good. Huh?" She was right. The map on the windshield suggested that she was smack dab in the middle of Huntington.

"You drive great," Dumphee told her. "In only a few thousand years, we'll have a traffic jam here."

"Good. I like jam," Lotsa Smoke said with a sage nod. "Strawberry."

From the back of the truck, Bear Tail levered the rocket launcher into position, nudging it just past Dumphee's cheek so that the experimental rocket pointed toward the windshield.

"Get that out of here!" Dumphee said. "What are you doing with that?"

"Me see heap big buffaloes," Bear Tail said, her eyes wide. "Me shoot 'em." She shook the rocket launcher threateningly.

"How big?" Dumphee asked.

"Big like trading post. Bigger than teepee."

"Big like hills! Big like hills!" Pretty Rose shouted.

"Bigger than the truck, huh? Did these buffaloes have huge tusks?" Dumphee asked. "With a trunk between the tusks, like on an elephant?"

Bear Tail shook her head no. "No trunk. Have tail on face. Animal all backward. Have big teeth, big like . . . taller than me."

She gave Dumphee a challenging look as if daring him to disbelieve her. "Huge teeth!" Pretty Rose said, all excited. "Bigger than tall pine trees!"

Dumphee nodded.

"Me shoot 'em," Bear Tail said earnestly.

"Only teeth not really teeth," Pretty Rose chattered. "Only look like teeth. Really, they two big pincers, like on back of pincer bug. And big monster buffalo, it pick up people, pick up ATVs, in pincers and carry them around to eat later! Oh, this terrible monster. Terrible bad. Manitou heap angry at us!"

Dumphee watched the squaws tremble with fear as Pretty Rose spoke. She was getting them all worked up.

"Oh, I wouldn't worry about those monsters," Dumphee said, trying to sound casual. Of course he was the only one here who knew that a mammoth wasn't likely to drag you off with its giant pincers and eat you.

"You seen 'em before?" Pretty Rose asked.

He considered. He didn't know the difference between a mammoth and a mastodon. Indeed, he'd learned most of what he knew about the creatures by playing with plastic toys as a kid—the kind of toys that come in a bag with forty extinct animals all thrown together. "Back home, we call them"—he searched for a word—"*grumpalumps*. But where I'm from they're extinct."

"Grumpalumps?" Pretty Rose asked.

"Yeah," Dumphee said, "the old punjabs, the grumpalump riders of Pern, they captured the grumpalumps when they were young and trained them for riding."

"How they did that?" Pretty Rose asked very suspiciously.

"Oh, it was easy. The grumpalumps had very tender feet. If you hit them on the toe with a stick, they learned to fear you. Eventually you could train them and ride them. Of course, you had to watch out for the wild ones. If they stepped on you, they'd squash you flat. And of course the really big grumpalumps, the imperial grumpalumps, were as tall as hills, and a whole village could cling to the hair on their backs and go riding off into the sunset. You could weave their long hair to make ropes."

The squaws had all stopped speaking, stopped breathing even, as they stared at him in rapt awe.

"You say these grumpalumps back home, they eh-stink?" Lotsa Smoke asked. "Smell real bad?"

"Not *stink*. They're *extinct*."

"What that mean?"

"Dead. They're all dead. They got killed long ago."

"Why you kill 'em?" Pretty Rose asked.

"They were too noisy," Dumphee said. "And they kept pooping everywhere."

Dumphee stared off, wishing this discussion would end. He didn't figure it would hurt to give Pretty Rose some of her own medicine, though he knew that if he kept lying so flagrantly, he'd eventually forget what he'd told them.

At least he knew now what time zone he was in. The Pliocene or Pleistocene or something like that. Cave men and mammoths.

Dumphee said, "Now, listen, I know those things are definitely going to go extinct, Bear Tail, so I don't mind if you shoot a couple. But you are not going to use the rocket launcher. You understand me? I don't want a rocket going off in the cab of this truck!"

Bear Tail pulled the launcher back under the canopy and laid it down, pouting.

Dumphee watched her from the corner of his eye, not quite trusting her. He couldn't help but notice the curve of her waist as she leaned away from him, or her long hair. All three of the women were decent looking, and Lotsa Smoke would have been considered stunning no matter what century she was born in. Dumphee almost imagined that he could learn to enjoy it here in the past, if they did get stuck.

"Ladies," he said after a moment of thought, "I think you and I had better get something straight. . . ." Lotsa Smoke slowed the truck to a crawl without quite managing to stop it. "We've gone back in the past, a long, long time. And . . . I don't know what kind of dangers we might face."

"Senecas?" Lotsa Smoke asked warily.

111

"No Senecas," Dumphee said. "In fact, I don't know if anyone lives here. Neanderthals, maybe. It depends on how far back we've gone, and I just don't know.

"But I do know that there are grumpalumps, and there are also some giant cats. Saber-toothed tigers, we call them. They're big enough to kill one of us and drag us off. So no one had better go too far from the truck.

"Beyond that, I don't know. We'll just have to find out.

"But our biggest danger is that time machine in the back, there. We can't bump it or move it. If we do, poof! Who knows *when* we'll end up?

"So, here's what I think we should do. I'm going to train you ladies how to drive and how to shoot. I want you to be able to defend yourselves. But I think that from now on, we need to conserve our ammunition. Understand? Don't shoot things if you don't have to."

With those words, he had Lotsa Smoke stop the ATV, and they got out in the dark pine forest, with the mist wreathing up from the grass.

Distantly, wolves howled, and a flicker bird flew under the trees, the white spots on its wings suddenly appearing in a slant of morning sunlight as it flapped between the black pine trunks. The ground was warmer than Dumphee had anticipated, as if the Ice Age really wasn't in progress. Dumphee didn't know what he'd expected. He'd figured that maybe all of North America would be a frozen tundra. But then he remembered from his geography class that he was near the Atlantic, and the warm currents coming up out of the Gulf of Mexico should warm the land, even now.

He got out an M-16, showed the women how to load, aim and fire it. Both Lotsa Smoke and Bear Tail took the weapon and blasted through some pine trees as if they were marine commandos. Pretty Rose feared the weapon, and would not touch it, though she was less timid when it came time to toss a grenade.

As for some of the experimental weapons, Dumphee didn't mess with them. This hurt the women—especially Bear Tail, who wanted to know how to use the rocket launcher.

"Look," Dumphee said, "I don't want you touching that. It's not for use on animals or people. It's made to shoot down airplanes."

"What airplane?" Lotsa Smoke asked.

"It's a flying machine with wings. Like our truck, only it flies in the air."

Lotsa Smoke studied his face, grinning slightly, as if waiting for him to break into laughter at his own joke. When he remained serious, she scowled, then slapped his face and pushed his chest, knocking him down.

"You lie! You think I stupid? You think I stupid squaw? I not civilize? I show you!" Lotsa Smoke scooped up the nearest branch from the ground and launched herself at him, slamming the limb against the side of his head.

"No!" Dumphee shouted, not wanting to fight. "I not lie! I mean, I'm not lying! Lotsa Smoke is smart squaw, very civilized!"

113

As quickly as her anger had struck, it dissipated, and she smiled. "You think I smart?"

"Yes," Dumphee said. "Very smart. You drive the truck very good. And, damn, you'd look fetching in a teddy. Very beautiful."

"Then why you lie?" she asked again, hurt.

Dumphee said, "I'm not lying. Here, I can prove it."

He raced to the back of the truck, reached into a box of grenades and found a user's manual written in Russian. He pulled off a page and folded the paper into an airplane.

"This is what an airplane looks like," he said, "only it is much bigger, bigger than the whole truck. You can put guns on the front of it, or have it carry bombs. And you put a motor on the back of it to make it fly."

He threw the paper airplane. It soared into the trees and glided a hundred feet.

The women's reaction was astonishing. Pretty Rose leapt and screamed in delight while Bear Tail raced after the airplane.

Lotsa Smoke merely stared at it, awestruck, then turned to Dumphee.

All the rage and incredulity drained from her face, and now she looked at him as if for the first time and said in unfeigned awe, "You heap big medicine man! You great brave! Good husband for Lotsa Smoke."

She threw him against the back of the truck, then kissed him passionately, her whole lithe body pressed against his. As she drove him back toward the bed of his truck, he knew what she wanted.

He kissed her firmly, ran his hands through her hair. Her breath smelled sweet. She squeezed him tight, and his heart hammered.

The first time he'd been with her, it had been with some reluctance, under duress. Now he wanted her fiercely.

"You never leave Lotsa Smoke," she demanded. "You never sell her. Okay?"

Dumphee imagined what it would be like, living back here. He knew from writing a report in the fourth grade that the last Ice Age had ended thousands of years in the past, and that men had supposedly found their way into North America across the land bridge at the Bering Strait.

But what if the reports were wrong?

Am I going to get stuck here? he wondered. Maybe all the natives on the American continent were his descendants. Maybe they'd be born from his marriage to these three squaws.

Lotsa Smoke suddenly began pulling at the ivory buttons of his uniform. Buttons she'd plundered from the trading post and sewn on the day before.

The other squaws saw what she was doing and ran to help. Dumphee didn't resist.

CHAPTER 15

Finding a way from Pittsburgh to Denver during the Pleistocene Epoch was not as easy as Dumphee would have liked, nor was it quite as hard as he had expected.

He skirted south through Kentucky and down into Tennessee during the next two days, traveling slowly over rough terrain. Yet as he crossed areas where he'd expected to find impenetrable forests, he found again and again that the trees were more sparse, more denuded of foliage, than he'd have imagined.

Huge animals had destroyed much of the woods.

At first, he couldn't quite envision what would have caused such damage. In a clearing he came across two giant bears that both stood, making themselves tall at the sight of the truck. They were short of nose, like the grizzly, and about the same color. But they stood nine feet at the shoulder and were very broad, heavier and taller than any modern bear.

Sometimes as he drove through the forest, he saw creatures that he couldn't name—beasts that hadn't been included in those bags of plastic animals he'd played with as a child.

When the squaws asked him what such creatures were, he'd answer quickly. They seemed relieved when he knew the answers and assured them that the odd beasts weren't really dangerous.

Pretty Rose spotted an enormous ratlike animal, larger than a grown boar, racing toward a river as the truck approached. "That's a Godzilla hamster," Dumphee answered when she asked its name. Giant rhinos with long mangy hair became "horny-hounds."

When Dumphee drove up to an animal that looked like an armadillo with a huge gray shell—a shell large enough to use as a tent—the creature hissed and batted an enormous armored tail. Dumphee had no clue as to what the animal was called.

"What that?" Pretty Rose demanded.

"That, dear ladies," Dumphee said in utter confusion, "is a being from the Eternal Pit. A lesser demon from the seventh hell. Back home we called it . . . a *fumigator*."

"Like alligator?" Pretty Rose asked, eyes wide. She'd apparently heard of gators somewhere.

"Like an alligator, only much worse," Dumphee said. "Its bite is poisonous. We'd best stay clear."

As he drove, he began to see what had so devastated the forests.

Woolly mammoths and mastodons were everywhere, in several different sizes and species. Dumphee didn't know if he'd landed ten thousand years in the past, or a hundred thousand. But it was a mastodon's world.

The mammoths were as different from the mastodons as a Guernsey cow is from a buffalo.

The woolly mammoths ran in herds of a hundred or two, and each adult mammoth was much larger than an African elephant, with tusks that curled in a great spiral, like the shoot of a fern as it comes from the ground. Their shaggy hair was a foot or two long, anywhere from reddish brown to almost black, and the mammoths had a distinctly odd profile. Their humped, sloping backs made it look inviting to try and climb one of the beasts, then slide down from the shoulders to the rump, and go flying into the air.

But the mastodons had much shorter, lighter hair. Their ears were larger, and their tusks were long and twisted elegantly, instead of spiraling. They also lacked the mammoth's distinctive hump. More importantly, they were nearly twice the height of a mammoth.

As they drove, Dumphee saw prides of huge saber-toothed lions and other cats following the herds, always shadowing them. The tawny sabertooths seldom hunted in packs of less than a dozen.

Once Dumphee stopped the truck to watch two huge mastodon bulls fight over a female. Each bull stood over twenty feet tall, and had enormous tusks, eighteen or more feet long. The bulls stood, tusks locked in combat, their massive heads swaying side to side as they trumpeted and tried to dislodge one another; nearby a young male practiced for future combat by butting a spruce with its head. As the tree came down, Dumphee understood why the forests were denuded and scraggly.

Dumphee had no idea how large a mastodon herd could grow. He felt lucky when he first saw twenty beasts together.

Yet as he came over a green hill near noon, he stopped the truck and stared in dazed shock at a little river valley, where the ground was almost black with mastodons, a herd of a hundred thousand or more, migrating north.

He'd heard of how buffalo on the plains had congregated in herds so vast that the wagon trains might take three or four days to cross through them. Such a herd of mastodons lay before him. He could not see the head of the herd to the north, nor the tail to the south. He didn't dare try to drive through it. One beast could bowl over the ATV, trample them all.

Shaken, he stopped at the top of the hill.

The air above the herd was thick with enormous buzzards with wingspans of fifteen feet, so that they circled like bomber planes.

"We go through herd?" Lotsa Smoke asked, worried.

"Yeah, maybe we sneak through," Pretty Rose jested.

Dumphee studied the situation. The gas tank was nearly empty. He had two hundred gallons of firewater, but that wouldn't take him all the way to Denver.

"I need to fill the gas tank," Dumphee said. "Cover me."

"Cover with what?" Lotsa Smoke asked. "Blanket?"

"Uh, just stand guard," he said, shaking his head.

He climbed into the back of the truck, wrestled a barrel of firewater through the canvas flap at the back of the vehicle, and stood for a moment, grunting and straining to hold the spigot up to the gas tank. It took a fair bit of maneuvering to steady the barrel enough to get the hooch in the tank rather than on his feet.

As he poured the firewater he stared at the great herd, wondering if maybe he shouldn't shoot a rocket down into that valley in the hopes of stampeding the mastodons.

The only problem was, he didn't have any guarantee that the whole danged herd wouldn't decide to stampede over the top of him.

Dumphee had just emptied half of the first barrel when the sabertooths struck:

He never saw them coming—only heard a terrified scream and some ferocious roars as lions leapt atop the truck and began slashing through the canvas tarpaulin.

Bear Tail shrieked, emptied a clip into the canvas above her. Blood rained. A tawny shape with darker stripes flopped to the ground.

Dumphee turned to see a dozen sabertooths race toward the truck.

He dropped his keg and rolled beneath the tires, thinking they were after him, but the cats leapt onto the tarpaulin.

Suddenly he realized that the cats had never seen a human before, might not even think of him as prey, but they'd mistaken the ATV for some kind of mastodon and were intent on bringing it down.

All hell broke loose.

Bear Tail was still shrieking, firing all over the place, and three or four cats dropped from the truck, blood spattering everywhere. One wounded cat roared and raked a tire with its claws.

The cat looked at Dumphee with huge green eyes; it saw Dumphee squirming under the truck. The sabertooth snaked its paw toward him, trying to snag him with claws as big as meat hooks. Dumphee was astonished by the cat's reach. It threw itself half under the tires and snagged his jacket.

Dumphee lunged back, clinging to an axle while the lion roared, its huge maw gaping wide, showing serrated teeth over a foot long. The lion pulled on Dumphee's jacket, yanking him close, and Dumphee struggled to escape.

Inside the truck, Pretty Rose pounded the air horn in three short blasts, then cranked the engine.

Just as Dumphee realized that Pretty Rose was going to take off driving, the lion roared and tugged hard. Dumphee's whole body was lifted in the air and drawn a yard closer toward the cat. He struggled to hold on to the axle with aching fingers, and dug his heel into the ground.

The truck surged forward, rolling over the lion's front paws.

It roared in rage as the truck lurched away. Dumphee struggled to hold on to the axle, but the cat's claws were still in his jacket, drawing him back.

He lost his grip.

Suddenly the truck was gone, leaving Dumphee to lie out in the open.

Dumphee shrugged out of his jacket so fast, that even he didn't know quite how he got it off.

He jumped up and ran for the truck.

Four lions clung to the canopy, slashing through it, tearing it to ragged pieces, their eighteen-inch fangs locked onto the struts that held the canvas. Their eyes rolled in their heads and their stubby tails writhed back and forth. Bear Tail was screaming in terror, trying to fumble a second clip into the M-16.

Meanwhile, Lotsa Smoke leapt out the passenger door of the truck, yelling, and raced toward Dumphee. He figured she was scared witless, trying to escape from the cats.

But Lotsa Smoke wasn't running madly away from the truck—she was coming to his aid, with nothing more than her commando knife in hand. She snarled at the cats, trying to face them down. She'd come to save him!

She grabbed his shoulder and tried to pull him toward the open door of the cab.

Bear Tail yelled and got the M-16 firing into the canopy again, blew a hole through a green-eyed sabertooth above her. The dead cat slid through a rent in the canopy and thumped into the bed of the truck. A second cat got winged and leapt away. Pretty Rose blasted the horn again and kept speeding forward. Two more sabertooths fled from atop the truck, obviously dismayed by the sounds and motion and their inability to bring the vehicle down.

Dumphee began racing downhill with Lotsa Smoke, trying to catch the ATV. Pretty Rose was trying to escape the sabertooths by driving into the mastodon herd. The cats feared the massed pachyderms.

"No!" Dumphee shouted into the back of the truck, just in time to see Bear Tail swing the M-16 in his direction. He dropped in terror, sliding over some straw stubble, as she opened fire. Bullets whizzed overhead.

A lion snarled in pain. A bullet hit the half-full container of hooch, and it exploded like a bomb.

Dumphee glanced back to see the monster cat still racing toward him. Bear Tail fired again. Her bullets connected, nearly ripping the animal in half.

"Hurry!" Bear Tail shouted desperately as the truck pulled away from Dumphee.

Lotsa Smoke grabbed Dumphee's shirt collar and yanked him back to his feet. They bounded downhill. Dumphee spared a glance over his shoulder. A dozen cats crested the hill, eyeing him hungrily.

To his amazement, he sprinted the hundred-yard dash faster than he thought humanly possible. He thought, I should be in the Olympics!

Even as he admired his own speed, Lotsa Smoke screamed in terror and bounded past as if he stood still.

A cat snarled at his heels. He didn't want to be last in line when it charged in for breakfast.

He and Lotsa Smoke vaulted into the back of the ATV and landed on a dead sabertooth. Dumphee felt astonished by his newfound leaping ability, too.

He looked back to see five huge cats racing toward the truck. They halted, dismayed by the mastodons ahead, and slunk back toward the hill.

At that moment, the stench of the mastodons assaulted Dumphee, an overpowering smell.

The ATV wheeled into the mastodon herd, crawling slowly among the young. Mastodons blocked out the sunlight as the vehicle moved in among the great beasts.

Pretty Rose steered carefully, trying not to get trampled, while looking every which way at once. Whole herds were snaking through this enormous migration, infants holding the mothers' tails. Dumphee desperately wanted to be in the driver's seat, felt he needed to be driving. But Pretty Rose was there, and he couldn't change places easily. He hoped the mastodons would mistake the ATV for a juvenile, as the saber-tooths had, and vainly wished that the truck could mimic the look of a mastodon.

He peered up through the slashed tarpaulin. Mastodons had small ears compared to elephants, and were more of a bronze in color, rather than the elephant's gray. It wasn't until he was in their midst that he began to appreciate their size.

The beasts overshadowed the truck. Their legs were so huge, Dumphee felt as if he peered into a forest of enormous trees.

But these trees moved.

The mastodons began to converge on the vehicle. Some trumpeted curiously as a couple of big females hemmed the ATV in and began letting their broad trunks play over the hood of the truck, gently smelling it.

"Come on, guys," Dumphee prayed. "We're just a little baby mastodon trying to find Mommy. Let us through!"

But the ATV wasn't a mastodon, and the herd mothers knew. The querulous trumpeting became frightened, and the mothers nervously stamped their feet.

A huge trunk snaked over the top of the ATV, came right down through a hole in the canopy and smelled the dead sabertooth.

The mastodon can taste the scent of the cats, Dumphee thought, realizing that this was bad. This was very bad.

A big male trumpeted. The mastodons moved closer, pressing the truck, hemming it in. One mastodon angrily slapped the hood with its trunk, as if having decided this ATV was definitely not a friend.

In panic, Pretty Rose hit the air horn.

The truck belched, and Dumphee prayed that it sounded like a wounded, dying mastodon.

Several mastodons backed away in confusion. Some nearby shuffled and returned the insult with blarings of their own.

A huge old bull, with enormous tusks some twenty feet long, set his ivory tusks under the ATV and lifted. Dumphee felt as if the vehicle was a flapjack and the bull's tusks would flip it like a spatula. He screamed as the truck lifted gently into the air, tilted to its side.

The contents in the bed of the truck—the barrels of hooch and the guns and Dumphee and Bear Tail and Lotsa Smoke and the dead sabertooth—all slid to the left rear corner. The time machine slid sideways and bumped the inside fender, but did not discharge.

Dumphee looked up through a slit in the canopy, saw the mastodon's huge bloodshot eye glaring in at him. The mastodon angrily trumpeted and shook the truck. Nearby, other mastodons heard the call to attack.

They trumpeted as they advanced. A female slammed her head against the back of the truck, rattling the vehicle.

Pretty Rose shrieked. Lotsa Smoke leapt for the tailgate, looking for a way to bail out. She muttered to herself, "Hit 'em on toes! That teach mean grumpalumps!"

She grabbed a tomahawk, preparing to do battle. Dumphee found himself crying a wordless warning.

Bear Tail opened up with the M-16, shouting some Mohawk war cry as she fired into the huge bull.

The bull responded by bearing the truck forward, and Dumphee knew that if he didn't do something, they would all die.

He booted the time machine, and heard an electronic whir.

I never noticed before that it made any noise, he thought, just as the peach-colored clouds enveloped them.

CHAPTER 16

The mastodon carried the truck through the mists, trumpeting in rage. Blood streamed from wounds in its head and trunk. It shook the ATV from side to side as if it were a rag doll.

When the mists cleared, the mastodon stopped.

It stood a moment, thoughtful, as if it recognized that it didn't have a hundred thousand buddies here to help out. Or perhaps it was only confused to find itself transported. It set the ATV down and apprehensively began to back away.

With a scream of triumph, Bear Tail shoved a new clip into the M-16 and opened up on the mastodon, nailing it between the eyes with a dozen rounds.

It dropped to its knees with a grunt, then heaved onto its side, its great legs faintly thrashing.

Dumphee stared through the torn fabric of the ATV's canopy at the marvelous creature, feeling sadness and awe. Such a waste. Such a sad waste.

He looked out the back of the truck. He couldn't tell at a glance what epoch of time he'd moved to, but he sniffed the warm air. A peaceful early autumn morning, with oaks and scrub brush crowding close, and a stream nearby.

It was impossible not to look at the little valley and remember how it had appeared when crowded with mastodons, how the naked hills had been filled with saber-toothed lions.

There was no sign that enormous feet had trampled this ground. No evidence that monsters had ever torn through this brush.

Are we back in the future? he wondered. He climbed into the front seat, took the Walkman out of Pretty Rose's medicine bag and turned it on. He hit the channel-find button.

Static. Still no radio stations.

The question was, had he moved forward in time, or had he moved backward? Dumphee looked around. A cardinal flitted through the trees and perched in a nearby oak.

No mastodons lived in this time period. The grass was too high. The trees too thick and tangled.

Forward, he decided. He didn't know how much forward, but he'd moved forward several thousand years.

And he wondered. If he had come forward in time, this was the first incidence of it. Every other time the machine had bounced, it had sent them backward.

He considered where he'd kicked the machine, the angle of the blow, the momentum.

If he had moved forward in time a few thousand years, he might be able to do it again. It was like that still his pappy used to keep up on old Bald Knob. Sometimes the hooch would get caught in the tubing, and you had to bang its side just right to get it running again. His pappy believed that you could fix just about any machine, if you only knew the right place to hit it.

Dumphee was tempted to kick the time machine again, but didn't dare. What if he ended up back among the mastodons?

He climbed from the truck on legs that felt rubbery and weak, then sat with his head in his hands for a long moment.

Lotsa Smoke, Pretty Rose and Bear Tail all began whooping in celebration. They leapt from the truck and did a war dance around the dead mastodon.

Bear Tail rattled her gun, shouting, "Me kill 'em grump-alump, big as hill!" She leapt about and began trying to climb the bull, and the other squaws laughed and raced to beat her.

It was a hell of a trophy, Dumphee had to admit. He'd seen some big ones down in that herd, but none larger than this.

And in the back of the truck, tangled among the jumbled boxes of ammo and whatnot, lay the carcass of a saber-toothed lion. It was huge. Fourteen feet from the tip of its nose to its stubby tail.

Dumphee had never been much of a hunter. Like every mountain boy in West Virginia, he kept a couple of stuffed weasels up on his dresser, and he had the antlers of his first buck mounted above his bed, next to the rack of a nice ten-point he shot four years later.

But as Dumphee stared at the sabertooth, he had to marvel. He gazed at its mouth, at its giant serrated teeth.

He shook his head in wonder. "Damned if I ain't gonna have you mounted in my living room."

He knew how to skin the thing, get its cape just right so that he could have it tanned.

The women were still dancing, and he shouted at them through the torn canvas of the ATV. "Ladies, we're going to camp here tonight." He looked at his hands. His fingers were shaking so badly, he didn't want to drive anyway. "Why don't you start carving up the grumpalump, there. Did I tell you I heard they were good to eat?"

Dumphee went to the front of the truck. He remembered seeing a tape measure in the glove compartment. He took it out and began writing down measurements for his cat—distance between the eyes, length of tail and back, and of each leg bone.

The squaws, meanwhile, set a fire and began butchering the mastodon, taking huge steaks off the backstrap.

By sunset Dumphee had his saber-toothed lion cape all rolled into a ball and the cat's skull resting beside it. He didn't like the idea of leaving the uncured hide out, but he didn't plan to stay here long enough to stretch and dry it.

He managed to chop through the base of the mastodon's tusks with a hatchet. With the help of the squaws, he slung the tusks atop the ATV, then emptied the kegs of firewater into the gas tank, and cleaned and restacked the back of the truck.

Afterward, Dumphee sat down with the squaws and had a dinner of what he figured had to be the finest oakwood-smoked barbecue mastodon steaks anyone ever ate.

CHAPTER 17

The next day they drove through what would someday become Kentucky, a land of bears and deer, streams and hills. Sometimes they passed Indian lodges, but on sighting the strange vehicle, the locals fled.

At mealtimes Dumphee and the squaws made a brief camp, eating warmed mastodon, before continuing their journey.

After sundown, Dumphee drained the last keg of brew into the gas tank. Because their camping spot was so infested with mosquitoes, he decided to move on. He let Lotsa Smoke drive into the night while he slept in the cab, resting his head comfortably against Bear Tail's shoulder.

Just before dawn he woke as the ATV rolled smoothly through a vast field of Indian corn, the headlights catching the multicolored kernels ripening fat on the ears.

"Where are we?" Dumphee asked.

"Earth," Pretty Rose said.

Lotsa Smoke's eyes were glazed from driving all night, and she grinned at him. "Manitou hear me! Me smart Indian. We at Great Rivers."

"What do you mean 'Great Rivers'? Where?"

"Me see from map. Over there is heap big river, Mississippi. Other one coming in is Missouri." She nodded out the left window, though Dumphee could not see anything in the darkness but stalks of corn and a little light on the horizon. Still, he looked up at the map that the computer shone on his window. According to it, he was south of the confluence of the Missouri and Mississippi—a few miles north of what would someday be St. Louis.

Lotsa Smoke continued wisely, "Up ahead, me see heap big lodge on hill. Me very savvy. This Fort de Chartres."

Through a break in the cornfield, Dumphee could indeed see the outline of a fortress on a hill against the dark sky. In fact, he could see dozens of small hills, each with buildings or flagpoles rising from them. But as he studied the land around him, he saw enormous walls all around the hills—so that the fortress complex before him appeared to be much larger than any fortress he'd ever imagined from the 1800s.

"Are you sure this isn't Camelot or something?" Dumphee asked. The fortress seemed odd. Smoke rose from a large building atop the hill, a building with a peaked roof. Dumphee imagined that maybe it could be a French chateau, but he felt apprehensive. Flagpoles stood before the door.

"Not Camelot," Pretty Rose said. "This place have only square tables."

"You know about Camelot?" he asked in surprise.

"Uh-huh," Pretty Rose said. "At missionary school, I read Malory—learn all about Arthur, and Merlin, and Lancelot. Heap interesting."

Dumphee smiled. Between Pretty Rose's wisecracks about Camelot and the Crusades, he was beginning to suspect that she had learned more history than even he knew. He'd seen her studying the mechanisms on the weapons, too, and trying to figure out how the M-16 worked. Though she was a savage, at the very least he was beginning to realize that she was smarter than he was.

"No, this not Camelot, this Fort de Chartres," Lotsa Smoke said. "We get much firewater here. You no tell them you English. This French fort, belong to French father over great waters."

"What do you mean, French father?" Dumphee asked. "We can't go into a French fort. They'll scalp me!"

"What you care?" Pretty Rose said, nodding toward his slightly receding hairline. "Your hair gonna all fall out someday anyway."

"French no scalp," Lotsa Smoke said. A sly expression stole across her face. "You act dumb. We say you Frenchie, no can talk."

The vehicle exited the cornfield, and there, not two hundred yards off, lay a huge field of short grass. Some fifty totem poles stood in a vast circle, painted in garish shades of blood-red, yellow and white. The perfect spacing of the poles, the perfect circle they formed, was somehow ominous.

Stonehenge. It was like the stones of Stonehenge.

To the north of this odd circle, houses suddenly came into view. Wooden houses with thatch roofs, unlike any Indian lodge or teepee that Dumphee had ever seen, yet also not quite like something from merry old England.

These homes flanked the sides of a large playing field, where poles with hoops were erected.

And then the sun cracked above the eastern horizon, just enough so that the walls of the city on the hill caught the light, and blazed in hues of gold and crimson.

Atop those walls, in small parapets, men began to wildly blow horns made of conches, so that a warning arose from everywhere.

The whole city was like nothing Dumphee had ever imagined. It wasn't Indian, wasn't European, wasn't Oriental. Yet Dumphee now recognized that the small, perfectly formed hills were too precisely formed. These hills had been made by hand—and the largest one was enormous, hundreds of feet high and a thousand feet long. Only a mighty civilization could have built this!

Lotsa Smoke hit the brakes.

In the dawn light, Dumphee saw men with spears, some twenty feet long, atop perches around the city wall. The blaring of horns filled the air. Women and children rushed from nearby houses, fled at the sight of the strange vehicle.

The ATV rumbled. Inside the cab, sirens suddenly blared, warning lights flashed on the panel, and a mechanical voice announced, "Warning! Warning! You are low on gas. You are low on gas."

Yet Dumphee's attention remained riveted to the fortress.

The truck's headlights were pointing down into the grass. Lotsa Smoke hadn't wanted to hit a buffalo wallow or run into a fallen tree.

"Flip on the high beams," Dumphee said.

"What high beams?" Lotsa Smoke asked.

Dumphee reached over to the turn signal, pulled back the switch, and light suddenly played all over the fortress up ahead. A huge gate had just opened along the southern wall, and hundreds of dark men in white cotton skirts were rushing out. They carried wooden shields and war axes with three or four copper heads on each axe. Some bore longbows and others had spear throwers. Their leaders wore faces tattooed like demons, painted in blue and yellow. Ornaments flashed golden at their ears. Some men wore hats of dyed porcupine quills, while others wore elaborate headdresses of turkey feathers.

Dumphee dimly recalled such dress from picture books he'd seen as a child. "Oh, no," he groaned. "These are Mayans or Aztecs or some damned thing. I never knew they lived around here!" Mayans, he decided. He'd have to call them something, and Mayans seemed the closest he could come up with.

All ahead, thousands of troops stood arrayed; the conches blew louder. One man rushed forward with a stick, on the end of which was a spear; he hurled the spear two hundred yards to thump against the grill of the ATV. If the truck had been a monster, he'd have nailed it right between the eyes.

Lotsa Smoke hit the air horn, and the Mayan warriors scurried back a few paces. As if the truck were a great beast that had just roared in challenge, the Mayans raised their shields as one and clapped their weapons to shield or ground, roaring their own mighty challenge in defiance.

Beside Dumphee, Bear Tail startled awake.

Lotsa Smoke's face fell in dismay at the threat issued by the Mayan warriors. At least five thousand men gathered at the south wall of the fortress, and more were rushing to the city's defense. To Bear Tail, Lotsa Smoke grumbled, "What you say? Maybe we should pray to Christian God after all?"

CHAPTER 18

In the rear of the truck, Pretty Rose scrambled for weapons, overturning boxes, tossing hides.

"They no look nice! They mean! Get rockets!" Bear Tail shouted, crawling through the back window.

"No, not rockets!" Dumphee growled. He reached under the seat, pulled out the M-16, checked to make sure it had a full clip.

At the highest point on the mound above the town was a great temple. Naked slaves rushed from it, bearing lit torches, followed by guards whose copper armor and golden shields reflected the light. Priests also rushed about bearing staves, their long hair and robes dyed black with blood.

A great chief walked among them, a man whose robes were white as sunlight, as was his hair.

Before the fortress, Mayan warriors began to sing, dancing up and down in a running motion. Several hundred fierce-looking warriors fanned out, ringing the truck in a classic bull's horn formation, six men deep. The front line held archers, still stringing their bows, while behind marched spearmen with copper plates fastened to their shields. Swordsmen came last in line.

All the men wore military uniforms: yellow cotton balls in their ears, and faces painted in red-and-black masks. Many wore copper necklaces and bracelets of shell, while the highest of the leaders wore headplates of silver or gold.

Atop the city walls, a war chief appeared, standing in a regal costume of green feathers, wearing a huge leopard mask of painted wood and a copper helm with flowing plumes. He bore an enormous shield made from hundreds of golden plates.

He shouted some order, raising high a ceremonial Mayan sword with a hilt of green jade and four golden blades, splinted together like axe heads.

Bear Tail raced to the front of the truck with some imple-ment—a black hollow tube about four feet long. She aimed it toward the lined troops and braced one end against her shoulder.

"Not that!" Dumphee shouted. "We don't know what it does!"

He swung open the door as Bear Tail glanced at the arming mechanisms, threw a switch and tried to pull the trigger.

Pretty Rose came out of the back of the truck with a grenade in each hand and hurled one toward the Mayan troops fifty yards off. The Mayans by the grenade glanced at it suspiciously, then fell back.

Dumphee bolted out his door, firing his M-16 over the Mayans' heads. He didn't want to get in a fight. He didn't have any gas to make an escape, and he had no idea how many troops might be inside the fortress. Even now, another thousand warriors poured from the gates.

As his gun fired, the Mayans took cover in exquisite fashion. There was no groveling or running. Instead, the shieldmen rushed forward and crouched, making a wall of wood and copper for others to hide behind.

A grenade exploded, throwing up dirt and rocks. The shieldmen held steady, as if they'd faced things more frightening than grenades.

Bear Tail took aim with the black tube.

"No!" Dumphee shouted, trying to pull it from her grasp. Given her stance, if she was holding the weapon backward, the tube would fire into the truck.

The tube discharged into the air.

In the dawn sky a single rocket arced skyward in a streak of red, going up and up. It popped loudly, and the sky filled with a shimmering image: an enormous American flag with the sickle and hammer where the stars should have been. The flag could not have been less than five hundred yards long. A bear ran across the face of it, chasing Ronald Reagan. From the sky, the strains of a brass band began playing the "Star-Spangled Banner," while an announcer with a heavy Russian accent said, "Throw down your weapons, running-dog capitalists!"

Everywhere, the Mayans stood gaping at the celestial image. Troops who had seemed supremely confident and well trained under gunfire now began to toss down their shields and weapons, prostrating themselves, crying out in prayer.

Lotsa Smoke jumped onto the hood of the ATV and began shouting at the men in Mohawk or some other Indian language, thumping her chest and making slashing motions with her huge knife. Dumphee had an idea what she was telling them; the last word she shouted was "Manitou! Manitou! Manitou!"

As music played and the scintillating flag colored the sky, the Mayans began to moan, crawling toward the truck with heads bowed. With each little crawling motion, they banged their heads on the ground.

Their moans became a song, a communal gasp, as they inched forward on their bellies. Yet none dared look at Dumphee or the squaws or the truck; none of them dared behold him.

"What did you tell them?" Dumphee shouted at Lotsa Smoke.

"That you God!" Lotsa Smoke giggled.

Pretty Rose grumbled, "Well, he good in bed, but he not a God."

"Great," Dumphee said in disgust. "That's just great."

From out of the fortress, the priests and slaves and guards now issued. Their great chief, ringed in torchlight, strode forward. He wore a robe of ermine over his shoulders, as white as his own long hair, and he held a scepter of silver inlaid with turquoise, with knots of white feathers on its head. His head-dress appeared to be aspen bark wrapped around a clump of white egret feathers. Golden rings glittered at his fingers and his nose, while gold shone dully from heavy chains around his neck. His face was a mask of tattoos—brilliant whites and yellows, with an image of a rayed sun on his forehead.

At his side several noblemen or counselors were dressed in robes of bright green parrot feathers that had to have been imported thousands of miles. Each counselor wore little breastplates of gold, and their cleanshaven heads were marked with detailed and magnificent tattoos. Beads of pink shell glittered at their wrists.

The priests walked behind the old chief, smelling of dry blood and putrefaction, exotic daggers of red and green obsidian thrust beneath their robes.

Behind these followed slaves—women who bore the torches, wearing nothing but an occasional anklet of shells.

Dumphee had never imagined pure evil. Yet he felt its presence now. He saw how the women were enslaved and kept naked. He saw in an instant how the rich lorded it over the poor in this society. The priests smelled of rotting flesh and had dyed their hair and skin in the blood of sacrifices. When Dumphee saw the hungry looks that the priests gave to the squaws, Dumphee feared that they sacrificed humans.

As the great chief approached, the people kept moaning and banging their heads on the ground, but now they focused their attention on the chief.

Dumphee saw that the chief demanded such treatment.

The old fellow walked through the crowd of groveling warriors, a scowl of outrage on his face. He seemed not to care that Dumphee was a god. The little show of fireworks had not impressed him.

The dozen naked women who walked behind the great chief watched him nervously, as if he might strike when angered.

Dumphee wondered why this old man was so out of sorts at being visited by a god. He could think of only one reason: because in this place, the *old man* was god.

The fellow shouted at Dumphee, pointing at the sky, as if berating him for making so much noise or causing so much trouble at such an early hour.

Dumphee asked Lotsa Smoke, "What's he saying?"

The fellow looked down at the ground, kicked dust onto Dumphee's feet.

Lotsa Smoke listened intently to the old man, then shouted, *"No parle Français?"*

The chief screamed what had to be some venomous insult and spat on the ground.

A war leader near the front rank of soldiers was still groveling; the great chief rushed over to the war leader, kicked the fellow in the side of the head and pointed at Dumphee, as if ordering the man to attack.

Dumphee aimed the M-16 halfway between himself and the great chief or god or whatever he thought himself to be, then squeezed off half a dozen rounds. The great chief glared up at Dumphee with pure hatred.

Dumphee said, "Go ahead, make my day, you Mayan son of a dog."

The old man held Dumphee's eye for a moment; Dumphee saw doubt flicker across his face. The chief shouted, made some wide gestures with his hands.

Suddenly, Lotsa Smoke began gesturing back at the old fellow, talking in sign language.

"What did he say?" Dumphee asked.

"Oh, he very mad," Lotsa Smoke answered. "He say *he* god. He say he Brother to the Sun."

"What did you say back?" Dumphee asked.

"I tell him that you the Sky God. You greater than sun. You Sky God who holds the puny sun in his hand."

The old chief looked stricken at the remark. He cursed more loudly and rushed toward Dumphee, venom in his eyes. He made some emphatic gestures.

"He say bad things about your mother, now!" Lotsa Smoke offered.

"Oh yeah?" Dumphee asked, he kicked some dirt on the old chieftain's feet. "Well, your mother was a troll, and you were fathered with the aid of a turkey baster!"

The chief screamed in wordless rage at the insult, though he could not have understood it. Still, Dumphee's tone had carried.

147

"You . . . impostor!" Dumphee shouted, spitting back on the old chieftain. Lotsa Smoke made some grand gestures, interpreting in sign language. "I'm more of a god than you could ever hope to be, you self-aggrandizing little coyote fart! Listen to this!" He pulled off a half-dozen rounds from his M-16. "Hear that? I carry thunder in my hands!"

The old chief shouted at his people, pointing back at the fortress. He kicked a couple more soldiers, making extreme gestures in the air.

Lotsa Smoke translated. "He say people go back home, or he tell sun to go away."

Uncertainly, the warriors began to rise to their feet. Some dusted off their fur capes and cotton skirts. Then they turned and ambled back to their fortress.

"Hey, where are you going?" Dumphee shouted. "I'm here to free you. Come back here and worship me proper! You see them teeth strapped to my truck?" Dumphee pointed to the mastodon tusks. "Those came out of my mother. She was a mean old snake, but I killed her and yanked her teeth out just the same. And I'll do the same to any man here who looks at me funny. You got that?"

Only the old chief dared look at Dumphee. The others could not have helped but hear or see him, but none dared glance his way or incline an ear. The chief leered victoriously, raised up to his full height of five feet one, and held his chin high.

"My name is Dumphee," Dumphee said to the old fellow. Dumphee pointed at his chest. "Dumphee."

The old fellow nodded, pounded his own chest with one hand. "Cahon!"

The chief turned to walk back into his fortress.

"Always pleased to make the acquaintance of another god," Dumphee said to the old man's back, as his retinue followed. "You think you're better than me, just 'cause you got a lot of naked women following you around? Well, my wives are better than yours any day!"

Dumphee looked over to Lotsa Smoke. "Well, what did he tell them?"

Lotsa Smoke sneered with contempt. "Oh, they ignorant savages. No speak good Mohawk. They too stupid speak French. No speak Iroquois. Not even speak Seneca."

"All right, so they're too dumb to talk in any proper language," Dumphee agreed. "What did he say?"

"Him use sign language. He say you no god. We devils. People no talk to us. No look at us. He hope we go away."

"Yeah, well, I wish we could," Dumphee said, "but we're out of fuel. This truck won't go more than another couple of miles."

Lotsa Smoke licked her lips. "Ignorant savages. They have too much gold." She eyed the fortress longingly.

CHAPTER 19

The ATV made it a couple of miles up the Mississippi before Dumphee decided to call it quits. Beside the broad brown river he found an old abandoned hut made of sticks and wattle, with a roof of reeds. It would have to do as a temporary shelter. Of course, the roof was caving in and full of holes, but Bear Tail shinnied up the side of the building and began weaving in new reeds that Pretty Rose cut by the riverbank.

Meanwhile, Dumphee and Lotsa Smoke wrestled the mastodon tusks down from the top of the truck and leaned them against the hood. Dumphee wasn't sure, but he figured that the sight of those giant "snake" teeth might keep the Mayans from making a midnight raid. For good measure, he took out the cape from his sabertooth and spread it over the top of the truck to dry in the sun.

Then Lotsa Smoke lit a small fire in front of the old lodge and began warming the leftover mastodon from yesterday.

The mosquitoes along the river were ferocious, only slightly smaller than hummingbirds, and Dumphee was glad for a little smoke from the fire to keep them at bay. A couple of Mayans came sailing upriver in a dugout, using a single sail made of deer hide. Dumphee wondered at this. He hadn't known that Mayans used sailboats. The boatmen wore blue cotton tunics. They carried no weapons. But Dumphee could tell by the yellow cotton balls in their ears, and by the facial tattoos, that these were warriors.

He grabbed an army bucket and sauntered down to the river's edge, as if on a casual errand.

"Hey there, fellas," he called as the Mayans neared the bank. Both men averted their eyes, terrified, twisted their sail and headed downriver at double speed.

"You wouldn't know where I might find a filling station, would you?" he called in a friendly voice. "Or maybe some firewater?"

The fellows hunched lower, hoping not to be seen. Downriver a mile, Dumphee could see lots of other boats. In one boat, men were tossing nets overboard. But they didn't seem to want to sail near his outpost.

Dumphee filled his bucket with muddy water and climbed back up the bank. Lotsa Smoke was halfway up on the roof of the abandoned building now, handing reeds to Bear Tail.

"These folks don't seem too friendly," Dumphee said. "Do you think they'll mind if we stay here? I mean, we're kind of trespassing, aren't we?"

Lotsa Smoke said in a businesslike manner, "You say truck no can go on. We fix nice lodge."

Dumphee gazed into the decrepit building through the open door. There was a wide bare floor of dried mud. No one had lived here for years, yet it looked clean and comfortable. He wondered aloud, "What if the owner turns up?"

"Then I shoot him, you eat him," Pretty Rose joked.

Lotsa Smoke said, "Nobody live here. Nobody care." She suddenly fixed him with an accusing glare. "You no make us sleep in truck, huh? What if it get cold? We need lodge. What if Manitou make another big winter? Ha!"

She got back to work. Pretty Rose said, "Let squaws fix lodge. You go hunt meat."

Dumphee was tired of meat. What was left of the mastodon hadn't tasted as good this morning as it did last night, and at the rate it was going bad, he figured it would make them all sick if they ate it again.

He climbed on the hood of the truck and surveyed the land. To the south were the mounds and the city. Farther still was St. Louis, and he could see puffs of smoke on the horizon where more Mayans lived.

Nearby, a footpath wound through fields of corn to a little village up north. Corn. Just corn, almost as far as the eye could see. A darker patch of pumpkins or squash lay at the edge of the horizon.

"Forget meat," Dumphee told the women. "Tonight we're having corn on the cob!"

He went to the truck, strapped on a side arm and pocketed a couple of grenades, then took a burlap sack, headed into the fields and began picking ears. They were small, with multi-colored grains—red and blue and brown—not at all like the big, sweet yellow ears of corn that would grow here a thousand years from now.

Some little kids came and hid among the stalks, laughing at Dumphee and throwing dirt clods. Dumphee figured they were just playing with him, so he rushed at some naked little five-year-old boy and caught him by the wrist.

On finding himself caught, the child looked as if he'd die of terror. For the longest moment, he stopped moving, stopped breathing. Wouldn't even blink.

Dumphee felt terrible. How would it be, to be touched by a devil? Dumphee wondered.

He smiled reassuringly and whispered, "You're okay, kid. I won't hurt you!" Gingerly, he released the child. The boy stood a moment until a high wail escaped his throat. He turned and fled.

Dumphee walked to the edge of the cornfield and picked himself a large yellow squash and some red beans.

By the time Dumphee returned to camp, the squaws had fixed the roof and were all dressed in white beaded buckskins. They had unloaded the truck, and had set out bolts of bright cloth, a bucket of beads, some spare mirrors, tin cups and other goods that they'd stolen from the French trading post. Now they loaded the items into large baskets. Lotsa Smoke put on a gentleman's top hat, worn at a rakish angle. Bear Tail wore Fugg's sunglasses.

Dumphee set down ten dozen ears of corn and studied the women. None of them would meet his gaze. "What are you doing?" he demanded.

"Go town, now," Pretty Rose said. "We here long time, we set up trade."

Dumphee knew they were after the Mayan gold. Maybe they hoped to purchase the city for $24 worth of glass beads. It sounded risky, but each squaw had a couple grenades tucked into her basket, just in case. In the long run, the squaws were right. It would be best if they could get along with their neighbors.

"Well, as long as you're in town, why don't you see if you can find me some Jack Daniel's," he grumbled halfheartedly. He considered going with them, but decided he shouldn't. He was the big boss demon, after all. The natives might not talk to him.

Besides, if he did leave the camp, it might get raided while he was gone. Still, his greatest fear was for the women. "Listen, you be careful. These guys might cut your hearts out and eat them. Those fellows with the blood in their hair: they're bad news. Just stay away from them!" Dumphee wasn't sure his tone alone could carry the terror he felt.

Lotsa Smoke shot him a confident grin. The others didn't even look back.

CHAPTER 20

At noon, Lotsa Smoke entered the Mayan city with her goods. She came in the western gate, the tallest and most ornate. The Mayan city was built to be most impressive from that direction. There were hundreds of small sailboats out on the Mississippi, and Lotsa Smoke imagined that when foreign chiefs sailed here, they would come upriver or downriver, sailing close to the great temple on the tallest mound. It was a humbling sight, with the huge city walls painted so brightly, the enormous mounds, the log buildings atop them with their tall thatch roofs.

She walked through the fortress gates, past guards who stood on parapets above with their long spears, gazing over the flat flood plain. The guards studiously ignored the demon squaws. It was as if the women were invisible.

The day was warm, with the afternoon sun beating down. Flies crawled over everything, and the city smelled pungent. Within the outer wall was a market, where hundreds of craftsmen and farmers had set up trade. Blankets of elk-and deerskin covered the ground, and little frames of wood sheltered the trade goods.

Here a woman sat next to a pile of gourds and yams, while another had huge clay jars filled with beans. Many sold cotton cloth dyed in bright colors, or clay jugs for drinking, or blank plates of copper, silver and gold, ready to be beaten into shape. Like the white men, they dealt in goods from distant shores— coffee and chocolate, medicines, snake meat and alligators and live opossums. Precious stones were abundant, along with bright paints and arrows, combs made of fish skeletons, fish hooks cut from agate, bright shells, wheat and oats and rye and barley and other grains, nuts, fresh blackberries and salmonberries.

Under one booth three old naked women had a couch and sat piercing young boys and girls with needles, then rubbing in dyes for facial tattoos. Elsewhere, old women chewed hides to soften them, or sat braiding twine or grinding maize for dinner. Some sold salt or garlic or other spices and herbs.

Everywhere were signs of war: fortifications; brave warriors in their leather jerkins, some wearing breastplates and carrying swords or maces. Old men with wizened hands shaped arrowheads and axes from stone or beaten metal. Young men wrestled and threw spears in fields south of town.

Amid all this, the squaws began to ply their wares.

Bear Tail had a little basket of glass beads and needles, thread and bright silk bows. For two hours she stood by the city gates, showing her marvelous goods to anyone who passed. Some people gazed at the merchandise from the corner of an eye as they hurried past, but no one dared stop and buy.

Pretty Rose had brought furs and bolts of wool cloth, and aromatic French cheese, along with pepper and salt and other spices from across the great waters. No one cared.

Lotsa Smoke's basket was brimming with combs, hairbrushes, hand mirrors and even more exotic items—perfumes, silk scarves, rouge and powdered wigs. Lotsa Smoke herself donned a fine beaver-skin hat.

Yet the people passed, all pretending that Lotsa Smoke was invisible. She would walk in front of them, wave her hands in their faces, and spray them with perfume. No one saw her. It was almost enough to make her doubt her own existence.

To make matters worse, old chief Cahon came down to the market square and stood glaring at her so much that she began to worry that Dumphee was right. These people would kill her. It was a creepy feeling, but she showed no fear. She was Mohawk, after all. Still she felt relieved when Cahon left.

Just before noon Lotsa Smoke saw a hundred warriors bring a few dozen prisoners into the fortress—naked men and women who had been beaten and chained together. They looked so downcast, so dejected, that Lotsa Smoke had to wonder. She had been taken slave before, too, yet she'd never been as drained of hope as these people looked.

Almost immediately, a dozen prisoners were cut from the crowd and herded up the highest mound to the temple. As they raced up the wooden steps, men at the temple beat drums and blew conches. Everyone in the market turned to watch.

One by one, the prisoners reached the temple. There, the priests met them. Cahon took a long pipe and ceremoniously passed it over the heads of the slaves, then blew from this pipe, so that a white powder hit each slave in the face.

Almost immediately, each slave staggered under the effect of the powerful medicine.

When the last slave had been drugged, the priests led them all near an altar before the temple, beside a great red pole.

The priests stood at the base of it, staring up, until the sun reached its zenith.

Then the priests laid a drugged woman on the stone altar, which was shaped like a jaguar, lying on its back.

The people in the marketplace around Lotsa Smoke burst into song, chanting in their odd tongue. Their bodies swayed, and their voices grew louder. Some danced, stepping from foot to foot, bowing their heads as they sang.

With an animal cry Cahon fell upon the woman, slashing deftly with his stone knife.

Lotsa Smoke stood in dumb horror, almost not believing what she saw. Among the Senecas, she had seen men tortured to death, had heard good Mohawk warriors cry out in agony as their will broke. Yet she'd never seen anything as vicious as this.

For twenty minutes, the priests held a blood fest. The poor

slaves who stood atop the mound were too drugged to run. Most were too drugged to even realize what happened to them.

When the ceremony ended, Lotsa Smoke found herself standing still in the marketplace, breathing heavily. For half an hour she had hardly dared to breathe. Silently, sometime during the sacrifices, the other squaws had gathered at her side.

Bear Tail tugged at Lotsa Smoke's elbow and whispered, "What we do now?"

Lotsa Smoke had no answer. Earlier Dumphee had teased her about the Mayans. She hadn't believed that they would be as dangerous as he'd said.

"I glad they no want me," Pretty Rose said. "Maybe it good that we demons."

Lotsa Smoke swallowed, found her throat dry, tight. She looked at the marketplace anew. The poor here wore no clothes at all but for a scrap of brown hide or cotton around the waist. They wore no copper earrings, not even blobs of colored cotton. No tattoos.

Lotsa Smoke had been wary all morning, and had taken no chances. She had avoided the vendors' stalls, and simply stood with her basket of goods, being ignored.

Now, a rich woman passed, one who wore gold chains around her neck and ankles and was dressed in a brilliant red dress.

Lotsa Smoke studied her with renewed greed. It wasn't right that such evil people should have so much gold, while Lotsa Smoke had none.

Lotsa Smoke stuck a mirror in the woman's face. She reached up to push Lotsa Smoke's hand away, then saw her own reflection, and was lost.

For an endless moment the woman stood gazing at herself, gently inhaling and exhaling in excitement.

Lotsa Smoke pointed at a gold necklace with blue gems, then signed to her, "We trade."

The woman slipped off the necklace with one hand and took the mirror. The gold felt heavy in Lotsa Smoke's hands.

Lotsa Smoke reached up to put the necklace over her own head when a warrior leapt upon her. Dumbly, Lotsa Smoke realized that the warrior had been hiding like some gossiping squaw, spying on her, trying to discover what mischief she might cause.

He shouted at Lotsa Smoke, spitting and cursing. He grabbed the gold chain, ripped it from her hand. In another moment, he was on the woman who'd traded. He grabbed the mirror, drove her away with a kick, and stood shouting.

A crowd began to gather around them, a dozen warriors with swords and hatchets, who waved their weapons menacingly and shouted at her.

In moments, Cahon himself came down from the temple. The warrior who had taken the mirror shouted at him, still terrified. Cahon listened to the fellow, frowned, then took the mirror and thrust it back toward Lotsa Smoke.

"No," Lotsa Smoke objected, grasping the necklace instead. "That not mine!"

With an imperious glare, Cahon threw the mirror at Lotsa Smoke's feet. The mirror shattered.

Lotsa Smoke shrieked in rage, heart pounding, blood rushing hot to her face. She reached as if to pull a commando knife from her belt, trying to warn him with a gesture. Cahon backed away, shouting for his warriors. Bear Tail and Pretty Rose, who had been standing twenty feet off, rushed up behind Lotsa Smoke, struggling to make sure she did not pull her knife.

"No! No!" Pretty Rose shouted. "No fight! We get in heap big trouble."

The squaws pinned Lotsa Smoke's arms back. The warriors around them moved in, as if for the kill.

Pretty Rose pulled a grenade from her basket, and held it up threateningly. The warriors backed off.

Cahon raised his chin in the air, puffed out his chest, and turned and walked through the crowd, guards and slaves in tow.

"Come on, we go home now," Bear Tail whispered.

"Not go," Lotsa Smoke said. "If go, he think he won."

"What do, then?" Bear Tail asked.

Atop the hill was a great lodge, larger than any Lotsa Smoke had ever seen. "I know," Lotsa Smoke said. "We walk through village and look at things. Maybe we find gold, or make trouble."

Bear Tail's eyes shone at the possibility. She nodded.

They made their way uphill, passing mud houses. Rich people lived up here. Lotsa Smoke saw many women wearing bead necklaces, and men with gold on their ear bobs.

163

They entered the huge building. It was very dark. Great cloth curtains hung from the walls. Lotsa Smoke looked up a flight of stairs to a huge stone altar. On the altar rested a statue of gold—a jaguar with its tongue sticking out, looking down toward the front of the temple. Its eyes were made of enormous green gems, while smaller red stones lined its mouth.

Two women, wearing only breechcloths, had just laid heavy gold platters filled with burning twigs beneath the nostrils of the golden statue. Now they bent before it, muttering and bumping their heads against the floor, as the men had done when giving reverence to Dumphee last night.

Lotsa Smoke wondered how invisible these women would think her. Perhaps if she simply walked up and took the statue, the Mayans would let her. They obviously were stupid people. She climbed the stairs to the altar. The two women shrieked and backed away, terrified to find a demon in the temple.

At each elbow, Pretty Rose and Bear Tail followed, both making small cooing noises as they eyed the golden statue.

The gold drew her. Lotsa Smoke found herself nearly running up the stairs. When she reached the top she stood, breathlessly gazing at the statue.

Bear Tail whispered, "Gold! Gold!"

Lotsa Smoke reached to touch the jaguar.

From behind the red curtains came a snarling sound. Cahon leapt out, glaring at her, his mouth twisted in rage. Once again, he'd been following them, creeping about. Lotsa Smoke felt angry.

"Why you so mad?" Lotsa Smoke asked. "I not touch it. Yet!"

Just to anger him, she touched the statue, fingering a grenade all the while. Cahon bristled at the gesture; he looked as if he were mad enough to tear her apart with his teeth, but dared not attack. To anger him further, she spat on the idol, then turned and walked from the temple with dignity.

Pretty Rose grabbed a large red clay pot full of wheat that had been set before the idol, and strutted after.

Cahon began shouting gibberish, and the priestesses rushed from behind the curtain and began wiping the demon spittle from the statue with their hair.

"What now?" Pretty Rose asked, fingering the designs in the clay pot. "What we do?"

Lotsa Smoke couldn't stand the thought of leaving the statue. She carefully placed her grenade back in her basket. She gave the squaws a sly look. "Nothing. *Yet.*"

CHAPTER 21

Dumphee had been sitting in deepest gloom, worrying. He wondered if he should try to get back home, wondered if maybe he'd be better off living here among the Mayans. It would have been nice if they'd accepted him as a god. But now he was stuck being labeled a demon, and that didn't sit well. He figured it wouldn't be long until some brave sneaked into camp and planted a spear between his ribs. No more demon.

Worse, it didn't look as if he'd ever get the truck to Denver. He didn't know what would happen to him now, even if he did. He'd lost Lieutenant Fugg, fired off some of the experimental weaponry. He didn't know if he'd ever reach the right time zone. Certainly, he was a long way from Denver, and if that machine did have some way to correct itself, to pull him back to its original time of departure, he didn't know if or when it might fire.

He doubted that anyone would believe his story even if he did make it back. AWOL. They'd think he'd gone AWOL, out on a drunk. But what had happened to Fugg? Murdered? Would they think he'd murdered his commanding officer? Even if he did manage to convince them that he was telling the truth—that he'd traveled through time—he'd committed other crimes along the way: robbery of a French trading post, polygamy, slaughter of an endangered species when he killed the buffalo. Hell, he'd slaughtered two animals from extinct species when he'd killed the mastodon and the sabertooth.

The more he thought about it, the more he wondered if he could be looking at serious time in Leavenworth.

As he pondered, he shucked ears of corn and boiled a pot of water. His mom had always said that corn tasted best when it was cooked fresh from the garden, before the sugars in it had time to turn to starch. He took the salt from the back of the truck—salt, he reminded himself, that he'd stolen from the French—and gloomed over his fate. He wished he'd had the foresight to steal some butter.

Dumphee salted an ear. The corn was so dry, it didn't taste any better than sawdust. He let it drop to the ground as he considered his next move.

The squaws came marching up the road with their baskets.

"Chief, we got have powwow!" Lotsa Smoke said angrily.

"Fine," Dumphee said, looking up without really seeing her. He was still deep in his dire funk.

"You say ATV no run unless it drunk on firewater. Right?"

"Yeah, we need gas or something," Dumphee said.

"But you say you know how make firewater!" she accused. "Why you no make? What need make firewater?"

Dumphee gazed into her eyes, then looked down at the boiling corn. Corn. Fields of corn for as far as the eye could see. "Corn, mainly," Dumphee admitted.

"Got plenty corn," Lotsa Smoke said in a sage tone.

"It's not just corn. It takes more than that. We need a still."

"Hmmm . . ." Lotsa Smoke said suspiciously. "What we need still?"

"A *still*, a machine to make firewater in."

"What this 'still' look like?"

"Well . . ." Dumphee said. He looked into her eyes thoughtfully. He'd already begun to realize that the squaws were smarter than he'd first given them credit for. Just because they tended to grunt a lot and didn't use many prepositions, it didn't mean they were stupid or uncivilized. In fact, they probably knew a lot more about *this* civilization than he did. At least they talked sign language. And despite the fact that Greece and Rome were touted as the center of ancient Western civilization, neither those countries nor all the European, Asian and African societies combined had come up with something as simple and useful as sign language to help break their communication barriers. No, Lotsa Smoke didn't just have normal intelligence, Dumphee decided. She was downright crafty. "Well, a still works like this," he said, picking up a stick from the fire and drawing in the dust at his feet. "First, you need a big tank to cook the firewater in—a tank you can boil." He drew the tank with a fire beneath it, wondering what he might use to make such a large container.

"Make sense," Lotsa Smoke nodded wisely. "Must put fire into water to make firewater."

"Yeah. Then we'd need some copper tubing, a long copper tube to draw the firewater out of the tank and into our jugs." He sketched the coils of the still, showed a jug at the end. "But this whole thing is huge!" Dumphee said, suddenly feeling hopeless. "It will take a lot more copper than we'll ever find around here."

Lotsa Smoke glared at him, her voice so low and menacing it sounded of deadly intent. "If no have copper, what else can still be made of?"

Dumphee considered. "Nothing, that I can think of."

Savagely, Lotsa Smoke leaned in, her face a mask of resolve. "You *think* of something!"

〜〜〜

That night as they sat around the campfire letting smoke keep the mosquitoes at bay, Dumphee listened to the lonely gurgle of the river, to catfish jumping.

His stomach, tied in knots, growled hungrily. Bear Tail looked at Dumphee in pity. She held out a piece of dried buffalo meat.

Lotsa Smoke, wrapped in an Indian blanket, looked up at Bear Tail and Dumphee menacingly. "You think of something make still?"

"No," Dumphee admitted.

"No can eat then. Not till think what still is made of." Under Lotsa Smoke's fierce gaze, Bear Tail dropped the buffalo to the ground.

⊓⊓⊓⊓

Hours later, Dumphee crawled under a blanket in the little shed, still trying to think. He'd considered everything to use as a container—sewn hides, a hollowed stone, a dugout of wood. None seemed practical. None would hold up under the combined stresses of fire and the weight of the brew.

He *could* take the gas tank off the truck, use the fuel line to make the coils, but he feared that in doing so, he'd ruin the truck. There were hoses under the hood that might work as coils—radiator hoses and whatnot—but once again, he feared losing them. No, it wasn't worth the risk. There was enough copper around so that he could make coils.

Still, the vats troubled him.

As he lay under the blanket, Bear Tail and Pretty Rose crawled in to keep him company. A pleasant diversion.

Lotsa Smoke shouted, "Ai! Ai! No! Get out! Out! He thinking!"

The sun shone fiercely. Dumphee looked at Lotsa Smoke across the fire and pleaded, "You might at least let me have some lunch."

Lotsa Smoke did not even see him. In her mind's eye, she saw only the golden jaguar.

Across her field of vision, Pretty Rose came bearing a red clay pot with a tall spout. She poured tea into a cup of the same clay and handed it to Dumphee.

"No bother him," Lotsa Smoke said. "No give food. He got to fast until he have vision!"

"I make heap strong rat root tea—it give vision plenty," Pretty Rose argued. "You see!" She shoved the cup to Dumphee. "Drink! Drink!"

Dumphee greedily took a swallow, then gave a strangled cry. The tea was hot enough to scald the hair off a pig. He spat on the ground, then stood and began choking. He flailed his arms. One hand smashed the clay pot, knocking it to the ground, shattering it. Hot water bubbled on the ground and steamed.

Lotsa Smoke watched him, annoyed.

"Hot!" he shouted. "Hot!" He stared at the red clay jug in wonder. "Wait a minute! Wait! This might do! This isn't some crummy sunbaked pot. This has been kiln fired, like the ones my aunt Rowena makes! This might work!"

"Look!" Pretty Rose said. "He having vision. See: rat root work every time!"

Lotsa Smoke rose from her seat, gazing at Dumphee cautiously.

"Where did you get this pot?" Dumphee shouted. "You didn't make this!"

Pretty Rose glanced back toward the city. "Savages make it. I steal from them."

Dumphee had found a vessel to make firewater in.

In her mind's eye, the golden jaguar reached out one paw and beckoned to Lotsa Smoke.

CHAPTER 22

It took hours to find where the red clay was dug: a huge pit beside the river, miles south of the mounds. There an old man worked in a potter's shack, molding red clay into ropes, then coiling them into large pots and smoothing the coils with water. A huge, round clay oven outside the shack served as a kiln.

As the squaws made their way to the shack with baskets of trade goods, Lotsa Smoke glanced behind and saw that her movements had attracted attention—again. A Mayan warrior scowled at them from atop a low ridge.

In the shack, Lotsa Smoke signed to the old man, repeating each word as she did so, just in case he spoke some Mohawk. "You teach how make pots?"

She showed him the things she'd brought to trade: silks, hats and spices.

He glanced out the door nervously. She could see that he wanted something, but dared not name a price. He kept licking his lips, staring at them quizzically, looking back to the door in terror.

"Look, I have heap-good looking glass." She shoved a mirror in his direction, followed by a top hat and a commando knife. At each item, he shook his head.

Lotsa Smoke began to despair. Nothing could convince him.

Just as she felt ready to shove a gun barrel into the old man's nostrils and force him to reveal his secrets, Bear Tail went to the hut door, closed the flap so that the room went dark, came back to the old man and stood behind him.

She leaned the weight of her whole body against him, her full breasts pressing into his back. She began to massage his shoulders. She whispered one English word. "Please?"

The old man grinned toothlessly, then stroked her leg, smearing mud all over it.

Bear Tail looked up at the ceiling of the hut with a bored expression.

⊤⊤⊤⊤⊤

Near dawn the next morning, the old man removed a huge pot from his kiln, and he laid it before the squaws, eyes glowing in anticipation. The women nodded enthusiastically. All three squaws had legs smeared with mud from the old man's groping, but he had revealed his secrets for coiling and firing a huge pot. One needed a very precise mix of clay and sand. And before it was fired, one had to wrap the pot with willow wands and tie them together to reinforce the clay, lest the pot fall apart before it could dry.

Now it was time for the squaws to repay the old man for his knowledge.

Pretty Rose stood at the front of the hut and began to do a little dance, swaying and slowly lifting her breechcloth so that the old man's eyes were riveted on her.

His mouth hung open.

While she held his attention, Bear Tail took a heavy pot from the ground behind her and cracked it over the old man's head.

He dropped with a thud and lay groaning as the women grabbed their baskets and rushed off.

⌐┰┰┰┰⌐

The squaws worked nonstop the next day. They dug a yellow brown clay from the riverside and baked it into bricks, then began using these to build a huge kiln.

Often they would look up to see Mayans watching them— men rowing past or hiding in cornfields to the north. At dusk Cahon himself came with warriors to watch the women work. The squaws had stripped down to breechcloths and breast-bands. Lotsa Smoke did not know if he studied for so long out of mere curiosity or if he had come to ogle.

177

So she smiled fetchingly and hitched her breechcloth high as she worked the mud with her feet, softening it before molding. Soon, Cahon's scowl seemed less ferocious.

But as Cahon left that evening, he shot one final glare of disapproval toward the squaws, and Lotsa Smoke felt a chill crawl up her spine.

Dumphee took to wearing a hat as hard as a turtle's shell on his head, and when he was not on guard with an M-16, he forced Bear Tail to march back and forth with an antitank gun.

When the kiln was nearly finished, Cahon finally seemed to realize that the women were only making pots, and he looked angry.

Perhaps Cahon thought that they were acting too much like people and not enough like demons, for now the old chief posted a war party of a dozen men on each side of the camp. When Dumphee went to the fields to get corn, the Mayans stood at the sides, scowling and fingering their daggers, as if to deny him entrance.

After two days, when the kiln was finished, the squaws began making huge vats. They coiled clay and smoothed it, then wrapped the pot with willow branches and hide to hold it together as the clay fired.

A thousand Mayans came to watch the squaws make their huge vat, clustering on tiptoe at the edge of the camp, peering over the squaws' shoulders. Many of the watchers were warriors, men with huge hatchets and copper breastplates.

Perhaps the warriors gave some of the common folk confidence, for women and children made up the bulk of that crowd. Or perhaps the warriors planned to screen their attack behind innocent bystanders. Even the old potter came to see what the squaws were up to, a frown on his face and a huge bump still on his head.

Whatever had drawn such a crowd, Lotsa Smoke felt uneasy. She got too many surly looks from the Mayans. The air seemed heavy with electricity, as if before a thunderstorm.

As Lotsa Smoke helped Dumphee and Pretty Rose wrestle the huge pot into the kiln, she glanced up to see a young brave at the edge of their lodge, ransacking her trade goods, trying to count coup on her.

Bear Tail had also paused to watch them heave the great vat into the kiln—and so had become lax in her guard.

"Aiii!" Lotsa Smoke shouted, pointing to the warrior.

Bear Tail spun and fired the antitank rifle. A huge shell exploded into the corner of the building above the warrior's head. Mud and sticks flew as the roof of the lodge disappeared in an eruption of fire and smoke.

The warrior fainted, and suddenly everyone was screaming; all the Mayan townsfolk raced away from camp. But several fierce Mayan warriors stood their ground, drawing war clubs as if they would not leave their fallen friend.

Bear Tail shouted and fanned the antitank gun in their direction, but she did not have another rocket loaded.

Lotsa Smoke decided it was time to teach these savages a lesson, to prove once again that she was a demon. Shrieking like a wounded animal, she rushed to the cab of the ATV, got out Dumphee's tape player, and pulled off the headphones so that the little speaker worked.

She rushed at the warriors, shouting and pointing at the box. She signed to the men. "I heap powerful demon. I keep the souls of great medicine men in spirit pouch. I always keep in torment. Listen!"

She cranked up the volume to let them hear the strains of the Charlie Daniels Band playing "The Devil Went Down to Georgia."

The men stared in abject horror, and many a brave warrior began trembling uncontrollably.

"You no touch our stuff. Or I put your soul in pouch. There you sing in misery, forever, like poor dog!"

With a curt bark from a war chief, the warriors backed away. Lotsa Smoke hurled stones at them till they turned and ran.

She went to the fallen warrior beside the damaged hut.

He was unconscious, just beginning to grunt and kick his legs like a dog that is dreaming. She put the tape player to the side of his head and held it as his eyes came open.

One moment he stared at her, eyes wide, and the next he was slapping at her and rolling to his knees, trying to crawl away.

She booted his hindquarters until he leapt up and ran, screaming in terror.

Lotsa Smoke watched him flee. His buddies had stopped three hundred yards downriver at the edge of some cotton-woods. They stared back at Dumphee's camp. Cahon frowned.

Dumphee, Pretty Rose and Bear Tail came up beside Lotsa Smoke. She licked her lips, considering.

"Not many days," Bear Tail said, voicing Lotsa Smoke's concerns, "before old chief come and slit our throats for sure."

⊤⊤⊤⫟⊤⊤⊤

The huge vat would need to cook overnight, and in order for it to heat evenly, it needed to be cooked separately from any other large pots.

As Dumphee baked the vat, he fooled with some experimental weapons in the back of the ATV long enough to find some tubing to use for the coils of his still. The weapon in question had several extremely long, thin barrels made of a plastic, and when you pulled the gun's trigger, some sticky stuff flew out the barrel and landed in a tree, looking for all the world like gobs of green snot.

With a little work, Dumphee separated the four barrels of the gun and twisted them into tubing that was functional, if inelegant. As he worked, he had Pretty Rose make a second, smaller vat, so that it could go into the fire as soon as the first was finished.

Then he taught the squaws the great secret of making firewater. "We have three vats, like this," he said. "In this first big vat, you put in the wort to let it ferment."

"Wart?" Lotsa Smoke asked. "I no got wart. My mother had a wart. You got warts?" She looked around desperately, afraid they wouldn't have the necessary ingredient.

181

"Not that kind of wart. The 'wort' is the stuff you ferment. It's like a paste. You put in yeast and corn mash and some water in this big vat, and let it just sit and ferment, maybe stirring it every once in a while."

"What yeast?" Lotsa Smoke asked.

"It's a germ, like a little tiny animal that you can't see," Dumphee tried to explain.

Lotsa Smoke stared at him, angry that he would tell her such an outrageous lie, and Dumphee shook his head, tried to explain.

"It's very small. When my pappy wanted some, he used to go out into the woods and find him some wild mushrooms—morels. The yeast lives on those. Then he'd throw the mushrooms into the corn mash."

Lotsa Smoke nodded. "You go find magic mushrooms. We get corn and mash for firewater."

Dumphee nodded. "Okay. So here is what happens: once the wort has gone hard—after, oh, two or three days—we take a bucket and pour it into this second vat, then start distilling the liquor. When the liquor cooks, it will boil down, and the alcohol comes off in the steam. But the first time it comes through, it's mixed with lots of water. So we cook it again, distill it some more, until just pure liquor comes out."

"This pure liquor, it be strong firewater?" Lotsa Smoke asked.

"Oh yeah," Dumphee said. "It will cook your eyeballs, all right."

⊤⊤⊤⊤

Dumphee took a gun while the large vat was firing, and hunted along the river for mushrooms. He came back near dinner, his eyes puffy and swollen from his long search, but he hadn't found the mushrooms he needed.

Just after sunset, under cover of darkness, the three squaws went to lie in the hut, feigning sleep. They'd taken care to see where the Mayan guards were posted, and after a short rest they dug a hole behind the hut and slipped out to the cornfields.

As wolves howled, they gathered ears under the light of a full moon, sack after sack, and carried their loads back to their lodge. By dawn the cobs were stacked two feet high in the shack, while the Mayan guards seemed none the wiser.

Dumphee got up at dawn and went off again, this time heading east across the fields to hunt for mushrooms in the woods.

All day the squaws worked. The big vat made pinging noises as it cooled for most of the afternoon, and Pretty Rose put the second vat into the fire. Meanwhile, Lotsa Smoke and Bear Tail cut corn from the cobs, then pounded the corn with clubs.

When that was done, Lotsa Smoke poured it all onto a huge piece of canvas on the lodge floor. All day long she watched the mound grow, dreaming of the golden jaguar, wishing she could get the mash brewing. The large vat cooled enough by sunset that she thought it worthwhile to go ahead and begin pouring mashed corn into it.

As she worked, Dumphee came back again and threw himself down next to the fire, weary. His eyes were bloodshot. Dirt and sweat stained his brow.

"No find mushroom?" she asked, worried.

"Not a damned one," he groaned. Perhaps her question spurred him to further work, for he got up and went to a copse of alders by the river.

Lotsa Smoke finished dumping the mash into the vat, then went to the campfire. She waved her hands over the fire, gathering smoke to her, and whispered a prayer to Manitou, asking the Great Spirit to guide them all, to help Dumphee find his mushrooms.

When she finished her prayer, she offered a second one up to the Christian God, just in case.

In the half-light she went to talk to Dumphee.

Dumphee stood, face hard, watching the last silver light on the horizon. A flock of mallards winged over the river, and bullfrogs croaked at the water's edge. He said, "I been everywhere. I walked through the woods until my legs are so sore I don't think I can walk another step.

"Some of the Mayan warriors started trailing me about noon. Maybe twenty of them. I couldn't hardly keep my eyes off them.

"But, hell, even if I could keep my eyes off of them, it wouldn't do any good. There just ain't no morel mushrooms around here. Maybe they don't grow here. Or maybe this ain't the time of year."

He sounded desperate, near tears.

Lotsa Smoke nodded thoughtfully, wishing she could help. "What this morel mushroom look like?" she asked.

"It's kind of grayish, with a spongy-looking top that comes up in a peaked cap."

Lotsa Smoke considered. She didn't know what he meant by "spongy-looking," but she knew what a peaked top was. Some of the English officers wore hats with peaked tops. Lotsa Smoke had eaten mushrooms like the ones Dumphee was describing—but that was far away, in another land, another time, she reminded herself. Such mushrooms were very good, tasting like young venison.

In fact, as Lotsa Smoke considered, she realized that Dumphee was standing on some of those mushrooms. She'd been watching them grow all afternoon, and planned to cook them up tomorrow.

She reached down and picked one. "Like this?" she asked.

Dumphee's jaw dropped so far, she could have stuffed a bullfrog down his throat.

"I . . . uh, didn't see—I mean, my eyes are so bleary—"

She didn't bother to mention that she couldn't see them in the dark, either, but she did wonder how many of these mushrooms he had walked past in the last two days. Stupid white eyes, no good, she thought.

Dumphee smiled broadly. "Thank God, we found 'em!"

Lotsa Smoke considered a moment. She'd prayed to two gods, and one of them had obviously helped. But which?

CHAPTER 23

Dumphee's morel mushrooms worked fine. By dawn, the mash bubbled furiously as it fermented.

Over the next few days, Dumphee and the squaws worked nonstop, making more vats to let the wort ferment, making more pots for the still, hauling firewood, stealing corn, grinding mash, dumping wort in the still, boiling everything off.

The Mayans came and harvested their cornfields, so that the pickings became pretty slim. Dumphee spent the next few days salvaging what he could, and almost got himself eaten by a black bear that had come up with the same idea. Fortunately, Lotsa Smoke had been nearby, and she shouted at the bear until it plodded away.

On the fourth day of distilling, the first few drops of whiskey started to drip into Dumphee's collecting pot. He dunked in a tin cup he'd taken from the trading post.

He took a sip. As his pappy would have said, the brew was strong enough to scour the smell off a skunk.

With watering eyes, he shook his head and breathed in and out through his mouth. "This, my ladies, is genuine 180 proof. And I am proud to say, I made it myself, without no revenuer tax stamps on the still." He handed his cup to Lotsa Smoke. "To American ingenuity!"

Lotsa Smoke looked at him uncertainly, obviously unsure of the meaning of the word *ingenuity.*

But Pretty Rose chortled and seconded the toast, "To Injun-ooity." The squaws each took a sip.

Five seconds later, the squaws were all squabbling over who would drain the cup.

"Okay, okay!" Dumphee warned. "You can all have a sip. But this isn't drinking whiskey. This is fuel for the ATV. And it has to get us to Denver. Understand?"

The squaws glared.

"Wow!" Dumphee said. "Now I know what Custer saw in his last moments on Earth. All right, you can each have a cup!" he grumbled. No change in their expression.

"We work plenty hard. One cup firewater not much thanks," Pretty Rose pouted.

"A cup a day, then!"

The squaws all began to beam. In a moment they began to race about, each searching for the biggest cup in camp.

⌐⌐⌐⌐⌐

It seemed to Dumphee that it took a long time for his barrels to fill. He tried to stay awake for long hours over the next week. As the brew came out, he'd pour it into the tank of the ATV. A hundred-and-twenty-gallon tank doesn't fill quickly, not when the whiskey is just dribbling from a couple of little spigots. It took nearly four weeks to fill the gas tank.

After the tank filled, he began to fill the kegs that the French whiskey had been stored in. Seven twenty-five-gallon kegs.

He figured that they'd blown into this village in late August. As September turned to mid-October, he noticed changes in the landscape. Leaves were turning, branches becoming barren. One morning a cold wind whispered through the barren cornfields.

At night, Dumphee often lay awake, listening to deer and roving packs of raccoons as they hunted for the remaining corn.

Winter was coming, a hard one. Storms brewed—gray clouds sweeping over the prairies, bringing great dollops of rain. The signs of impending winter made Dumphee feel uneasy, bleak.

Yet, even with the steadily darkening skies, the squaws never over-indulged in whiskey until the load was nearly full.

Then one cold morning, Dumphee noticed Bear Tail on guard, sitting at her post on top of the hood of the truck, carrying the antitank gun. She wore his helmet, and had strapped some eagle feathers and beads onto the back of it. She had on her full buckskins, as usual lately, but she'd also slung his web holster over her shoulder. A forty-five-caliber revolver was tucked into the holster, while a naked tomahawk was shoved into her belt.

All normal attire, for the past few days. But something seemed wrong. He studied her.

It was her posture. Bear Tail sat with her head down, one hand close to her belly as if she were sick. Her eyes looked bloodshot.

He sneaked up close, and a woman who could normally hear a blade of dry grass snap at a hundred yards didn't even notice him. "How's the hangover this morning?" he asked loudly.

Slowly, with all the ponderous motion of a sloth, she turned to fix him with a hateful glare.

Over by the still, Lotsa Smoke was dumping the last wort into one of the vats. She began to giggle.

"And what are you laughing at?" Dumphee demanded.

"Nothing!" Lotsa Smoke snorted. "I just so happy today. So happy, you get firewater, go Denver. There we all be so happy!"

On the far side of the truck, hidden from his view, Pretty Rose guffawed, then burped.

"Yeah," Dumphee said, coming up with a sudden inspiration that might really get the squaws excited, "Denver is a great place. Out there you don't have to make firewater. It flows out of the burning mountains, all natural, in rivers and streams. Why, out there, firewater is so common, folks drink it morning, noon and night."

Lotsa Smoke stared at him, incredulous. "Why you no tell us this before?"

"I was afraid," Dumphee said, "afraid you'd all run off to Denver without me, when obviously it will be so much easier to go in the ATV."

With that, even Bear Tail suddenly threw herself into frenzied motion, looking for more corn to grind into mash.

⌐╥╥╥⌐

That afternoon, the Mayans decided to get mean again.

A storm was brewing, gray clouds blowing from the southeast, full of rain. Restless geese flew downriver in huge Vs.

Five hundred warriors came marching toward the camp in ranks, some proud war leader at their front. Dumphee suspected that he had to be part of the royal family, because he wore the sun emblem tattoo on his forehead.

They had bows at ready, spearmen and shield bearers, and men blowing conches.

As they drew near, Dumphee went for his M-16, figuring that maybe this time he'd have to actually shoot some of the fellows.

But as the five hundred men closed, Lotsa Smoke began talking in sign language.

She asked, "What you braves do? Why come bother heap big Sky God?"

The Mayan war leader pointed at the darkening sky, then replied in sign, "Darkness comes. The sun hides itself. Maybe it go away, not come again. The sun angry at us. We must make peace with it." He pointed at Lotsa Smoke and signed, "You come."

As Lotsa Smoke translated, Dumphee felt his stomach churn. He'd suspected that the Mayans would eventually want a sacrifice.

"Tell them that the sun is not angry," Dumphee said. "I am the Sky God, and the sun is happy. Right now, it visits longer in other lands, far away, so that people there can enjoy its warmth. But it will return soon."

Lotsa Smoke nodded sagely. She winked, as if he'd come up with a good lie, then relayed the message.

"Him no god!" the war chief signed vehemently, pointing at Dumphee.

"Him god," Lotsa Smoke said aloud as she signed. "Heap power over sky and fire and water. Me show you."

She went to a barrel, took a ladle, scooped up some fresh water, then carried it to the Mayan chief. He sniffed it suspiciously, took a drink.

"That water!" Lotsa Smoke said in sign. "Watch."

She went back to the water barrel, picked up a half keg

of whiskey next to it, carried it to the chief and poured it on the ground at his feet.

When she finished, the war chief stared at her.

"Hey, don't waste that!" Dumphee said.

Lotsa Smoke said to Dumphee, "Chief, bring match and light firewater."

Dumphee got some matches from the back of his truck. It was a French match from the trading post, a foot in length and all wrapped in paper to keep it from exploding when bumped, nothing like the safe little matches that would be used two hundred years later.

Dumphee unwrapped it, then struck the match. It exploded into a blaze. The Mayans gasped and looked at it suspiciously. He tossed the match to the ground at the war chief's feet. The whiskey burst into a great fireball that roared up fifteen feet in the air. The Mayans fell back, crying out in dismay.

"See!" Lotsa Smoke signed. "Him great god! You make him angry, he make whole river burn!" She waved her right arm out to the Mississippi. The war chief's eyes grew wide. "You make him angry," Lotsa Smoke shouted, "and he make rain turn to fire as it fall from sky!" She pointed to the great thunderheads rolling in.

Just then lightning flashed, and thunder cracked across the river. All five hundred warriors shrieked and fled, leaving their leader to take the brunt of Dumphee's wrath.

The great chief stood, his face a mask of terror, trying to figure out how to escape gracefully. "You make Sky God very angry!" Lotsa Smoke signed. "You give present, maybe him not be so mad!"

"Gift?" the war chief signed back.

Lotsa Smoke pointed to the armored vest he wore, with the golden plates sewn on, and to the golden armbands. "Him like that. You give him gift, maybe he not burn you up. Maybe he spare you. Maybe he spare all people."

The chief signed back, "Sun metal?"

"Yes, god like sun metal."

Quickly the war chief threw down his breastplate and armbands, pulled off the gold band from his head and tossed it down, along with a little half cape made of beaded buckskin.

Then he turned and feigned great dignity as he stalked off on shaky legs.

"What's this?" Dumphee asked. "Is he giving us this gold?"

"Hiiyah!" Lotsa Smoke cried, and the war chief turned stiffly.

She made some vicious hand gestures, and the war chief trembled. He made some signs, then fled.

"What—what did he say?" Dumphee asked.

"I tell him you not pleased with gift. It too small. I tell him you very angry, gonna make fire fall from sky if he no go back to city and bring all gold! Must have here by dawn."

She cackled between her teeth.

Dumphee stared at her in astonishment, hurt.

"You shouldn't have done that," he said. "It isn't right to take advantage of folks, just because they don't know as much as you do. I'm . . . I'm ashamed of you for that. . . ."

CHAPTER 24

Dumphee went to hunt some game, feeling troubled, wanting to be alone for the evening to think. Lotsa Smoke's greed disturbed him.

His fuel tank was full, and in another day he would cap off the last barrel of brew. But he was dismayed by what had happened this afternoon.

The "gift" of the golden headband and breastplates had left him in awe. He had been truly overjoyed to have it. Yet he felt . . . dirty, defiled. It had been so easy, so dishonest, and if the squaws kept up their little plot, he'd end up with a lot more.

"'Power tends to corrupt and absolute power corrupts absolutely,'" he grumbled.

It would be easy to live here among the Mayans, to take the place of Cahon. He'd seen some mighty fetching women back in town, and it was obvious that Cahon got his pick of naked women to serve him. He'd also have the best food, the gold; and he kind of liked the idea of being worshiped by thousands of people.

Dumphee tried to imagine sitting on Cahon's throne. He could gorge himself, satisfy every lust, live like a god.

Yet if he did, he could never quite be human. He'd never have the love of one good woman, or have the respect of someone who was his equal. He'd be untouchable, alone.

He imagined the things he could do as a god. He imagined what this land would be like if the Mayans drained the borrow pits where they had taken soil to build their mounds. These pits had become small lakes behind the town. Draining them would get rid of some mosquitoes. He suspected that there were a lot of diseases here that a little modern medicine could cure.

What would happen if he went back to the future, got as much penicillin as a truck could hold, then came back? He could be a god, a benevolent god who actually healed the sick. He could get modern seeds and fertilizer, increase the production on the farmland. He could get modern weapons. He had no idea what year this might be. What could the Mayans do with real guns? Right now back in Europe, folks might be fighting the Mongol hordes; or the Romans might have their crumbling empire sucking northern Europe dry of gold; or maybe the Black Plague was sweeping through villages, carried on the backs of rats, so that lonely bells tolled the numbers of the dead night and day; or maybe the Moslems in Jerusalem were falling beneath Christian swords.

It was a cruel world in this time zone. A world begging for order and a strong hand. A world that Dumphee could tame, if only he would take power.

But he knew it would not be easy. One cannot just seize a world and then walk away. One had to take control, to shape it, over decades. To do this would require great effort.

Dumphee wondered what was right; he wished that the old cave preacher from back in the mountains in West Virginia were here.

Then he got another idea. What if it wasn't A.D. 1000? He really didn't know how long ago the Mayans might have been in America. What if it was A.D. 25? What if he went to Jerusalem and found Jesus, then asked him what to do? Of course, he'd have to learn Hebrew or Arabic or something so that Jesus could understand his questions.

Or what if he even went to Jerusalem and stopped the Romans from crucifying Jesus? He could make Jesus one of his court counselors—or maybe get Plato or Socrates or Einstein to advise him. What might happen then?

All these questions whirled round and round in Dumphee's head, dizzying him as he pondered the possibilities, until he reached a small hill and looked down over the fields.

He pulled the Russian rifle he'd been carrying from its case. It was the fanciest danged weapon he'd ever imagined. It had an infrared spotting scope, a huge thing on the barrel that looked like a silencer, and its own electronic control panel. A tripod in the case allowed him to set the rifle up sniper style, while some little radar or sonar antenna spun around on top of the weapon doing who knows what. It was a motion detector, he decided, though it might be there to pick up or jam enemy radio transmissions.

For several long hours he just sat on the hill, watching a pond down beneath him, the radar antenna spinning around. Clouds whirled overhead. It was noisy here in the night. Crickets and katydids made low chirping and buzzing sounds in the grass, and somewhere in the fields, a wildcat snarled. Burrowing owls and screech owls made a fierce racket, and, once, Dumphee thought he heard a woman scream. Perhaps some Mayan woman in labor.

⌐⊓⌐

Dumphee hadn't gone a hundred yards from camp before Pretty Rose was into the firewater, trying to take the edge off this morning's hangover. She ran down to the riverbank and got a reed, then brought it up, stuck it into the gas tank of the ATV and took a few sucks. It was too dangerous to drink from the barrels: Dumphee always checked those.

Lotsa Smoke watched her a long moment, wondering at the propriety of drinking this evening. The storm was advancing, and the skies had gone terribly dark. Lotsa Smoke had managed to scare the Mayans off, but in time they'd return. It was best for them all to stay on guard.

Bear Tail had taken her usual position, squatting atop the truck with an M-16. But someone needed to watch her back. Lightning grumbled far to the south.

No, Lotsa Smoke decided. The Mayans wouldn't return tonight. They would stay afraid—with the threat of fiery rain falling upon their homes.

Lotsa Smoke felt terrible. She'd disappointed Dumphee. Maybe she'd ruined things. Maybe he'd never like her again. Maybe he'd even sell her to the Mayans or something.

Yet she couldn't help it. She wanted that gold like she'd never wanted anything before, and tomorrow Dumphee planned to leave it all behind.

Bear Tail joined Pretty Rose for a drink, sucked up the burning whiskey through a reed, and in minutes she was giggling and lightheaded.

That's when Lotsa Smoke began giggling, too, and gathered them together. "Shhh . . ." she whispered. "I have plan, make Dumphee very happy."

CHAPTER 25

While Dumphee waited for a deer to come down to the pond, a pack of coyotes prowled the water's edge, hunting mice and newts, then raced off to the east. Dumphee fiddled with the gun knobs, trying to figure out how the sights worked, not really sure what these fancy electronic things would do.

At long last, a pair of young does and a fine buck ventured from the forest and crept to the water's edge. Through the infrared scope, he could see the heat of their bodies perfectly.

Dumphee aimed the cross hairs of his scope at the neck of the huge buck, hoping not to spoil any meat, and held his breath as he squeezed the trigger.

Suddenly, in front of the buck, a waggling tongue appeared in midair, barking a noise that sounded like a

Russian version of "Nyah, nyah, nyah!" followed by a very rude fart.

The buck leapt in the air and jumped a few paces, then stood staring where the apparition had appeared, ears twitching in confusion.

"Damn," Dumphee shouted. "What is this Russian junk?" Some kind of experimental nonlethal weapon? What in the hell is this supposed to be good for? He was fed up. Every time he fired one of these Russian wonder-weapons, it turned out to have some use he couldn't imagine.

He sighted on the buck again, pulled off another shot, hoping that this time a bullet would emerge. Instead, a fiery phoenix bird began screaming in circles around the buck's head. A third shot provided a giant yellow armadillo that merely burped, while a fourth shot produced a towering image of Richard Nixon waving his fingers in peace signs and singing Creedence Clearwater Revival's "Bad Moon Rising." He was dressed in nothing but a pair of boxer shorts with little red hammers and sickles and green dollar signs on them.

By the time Nixon faded, the deer were long gone, and Dumphee had wasted the better part of the night sitting here. It looked like he'd have corn and beans for dinner tomorrow.

As he stalked back to camp, he noticed right off that something was wrong: the truck and everything in it was gone.

The campfire had burned low. Only a few coals still glowed. Dumphee hid in the dark and stared for a long time, hoping that the squaws had gotten themselves drunk in his absence and driven off to sober up.

They obviously weren't in the camp, and he feared that the Mayans had them. Everything was absolutely still.

Dumphee picked up his experimental Russian infrared rifle and played it across the scene ahead.

He spotted Mayans south of the camp. A little group of them, a dozen men sleeping in the grass by the riverbank beneath a knot of cottonwood trees. He adjusted the magnification. The squaws weren't with them.

Dumphee's throat felt dry; his heart pounded. He didn't have anything but this damned worthless nonlethal weapon. He began to worry about the squaws. They might be dead by now, sacrificed atop the temple mound.

He pictured Lotsa Smoke's beautiful face, felt a great hollowness in his chest as he imagined living without her. He thought of Bear Tail, her stoic nature, the way he'd always been able to trust her with the weapons. Or Pretty Rose, with her wry wit and willing hands, always the first to pitch in and get to work when work needed doing.

In a burning rage, he pointed the weapon at the Mayans sleeping in the trees and fired.

Suddenly, amid the Mayan camp, Joseph Stalin appeared in flames, shouting curses in Russian, while miniature Elvis Presleys writhed like demons at his feet.

The Mayans leapt up, shrieking and wetting themselves as they sought to retreat.

Dumphee realized that each image the weapon had created had been larger than the last, each a bit more mesmerizing or horrifying. He aimed another round at the fleeing Mayans. A three-hundred-foot-tall image of a brightly lit Statue of Liberty appeared, waving a giant mace as big as the ball from a wrecking crane and smashing at the ground with it, shouting, "Fee, fi, fo, fum, give me all of your bubble gum!"

The Mayans scattered from beneath her feet like roaches, and surely if Miss Liberty had been real, the Mayans would have died under the impact of her blows.

As it was, no human voice was ever meant to have screamed quite as loudly as these Mayans did now; Dumphee felt sure that some of them would end up mute from this experience.

As they all high-tailed it through the woods, Dumphee screamed, "Run you bastards! Run! 'Cause you have royally pissed off a god, and I'm coming for you now!"

CHAPTER 26

Bear Tail hurled a rope of twisted vine over the adobe-covered wall to the Mayan city, made sure that the grappling hook caught, and then drunkenly clambered up and over. The shadows were deep here tonight, with the clouds obscuring moon and stars. In moments she made a noise like the croaking of a frog.

Pretty Rose snickered at the sound, stifled a belch, and then followed.

When she was up, Lotsa Smoke tied the rope around the first barrel of firewater and heaved. The other squaws pulled it into the city, then they threw the rope back over the wall, croaked like a frog and chirped like a cricket, and Lotsa Smoke sent up the second barrel of firewater, and at last hurried over.

She leapt down from the wall. It was growing late, and very little light shone within the Mayan city—only a few stray rays from campfires within the huts, and these shone out only when the woven mats that covered the windows were tied up. Given the blustery night, most of the mats were down, and the city was shut tight. Lightless.

But up on the tallest mound, where the temple stood with its single huge red lodge pole, hundreds of Mayans had gathered. There they pounded drums and danced war dances.

The squaws laid the heavy barrels of firewater on their sides, and Pretty Rose sat down on one, still chirping like a drunken cricket.

Bear Tail howled like a coyote.

"Oh, shut mouths!" Lotsa Smoke said. "You gonna get us heap trouble."

Bear Tail fell on the ground laughing, and a couple of grenades rolled from her pockets. Lotsa Smoke grabbed the grenades, shoved them back in and pushed Bear Tail upright.

Then she aimed the two drunken squaws toward the highest mound in the city, and said, "Take firewater there, go back way!"

Pretty Rose and Bear Tail laughed and grunted, and began rolling the barrels along. Lotsa Smoke watched them stagger off and shook her head, afraid they would get caught.

Lotsa Smoke herself crouched low, then began weaving through the city, moving stealthily from shadow to shadow.

There were dozens of streets and perhaps a thousand huts here within the walls. Most of the finer huts were situated on low mounds, high enough so that even if the Mississippi flooded in midwinter, the huts would be high and safe above the water. But the smaller huts of the poor were clustered in low spots, close to the streets, and Lotsa Smoke crept along in the shadows of these huts, until she reached the central square beneath the mound.

There, to her surprise, she saw the war chief who had visited them earlier in the night. He was tied between two poles, his hands raised up painfully, and looking as if he had been beaten. He moaned softly. At his feet was the glitter of gold.

Instinctively, Lotsa Smoke knew what had happened. He had come back to the city and carried his message, the threat of Dumphee's wrath upon the city, and sought to get the gold to save his people.

But Cahon objected. So he'd had the man tied and beaten, then thrown gold at his feet as a gesture of humiliation. Lotsa Smoke crept across the dark square, and found bracelets and earrings and nose rings by the score. She found daggers and small statues. In moments she had a hundred pounds of gold in a bag, but it wasn't enough. One thing remained to be taken.

The war chief moaned, opened his eyes. He saw her crouched there on the ground and spoke some imploring words. Lotsa Smoke did not understand them, but she pulled out her knife, cut the hide ropes that held the man's wrists and let him fall to the ground.

Then she scurried off back into the shadows, hurrying beneath some of the smaller mounds to the base of the great mound.

Four separate trails led to its top—one each from the east, west, north and south. On the west side of the great mound, the warriors danced and cavorted around a great bonfire, waving their battle-axes and banging on shields. They did not notice one single squaw swiftly leaping up the south steps.

Lotsa Smoke reached the top of the mound and went to the huge temple. Cahon said that he was a god, Brother to the Sun, and so she reasoned that he would have his room on the east, where he could watch his brother leap into the sky at dawn. She crept round the side of the temple, until she reached the east, and then she looked in each window.

It did not take long to find Cahon. His window was open and a small fire burned in his room. He sat at a table covered with clay pots, and he was rubbing red grease onto his hands and arms. A huge ceremonial jaguar mask, made of silver and covered with jade, lay on the table next to him, along with a black robe.

No one was in the room with him. Lotsa Smoke studied him for a moment, reached into her bag of gold artifacts and pulled out a little figurine of a Mayan fertility goddess, a woman with her legs splayed wide, a swollen belly and long pointy breasts. She hefted it. The figurine was small but had to weigh five pounds.

She peeked back into the window, cocked her arms and whispered, "Pssst, Cahon."

Cahon whirled toward her, a scowl on his face, as if he would snarl at her for daring to disturb him.

The fertility goddess hit him right between the eyes, and he bowled over in his chair.

Lotsa Smoke leapt through the window, found Cahon still breathing. She gagged him and tied him to his chair, then quickly began painting her own hands with red grease.

An hour later, Cahon strode into the temple dressed in his black ceremonial robes and jaguar mask. With him came two acolytes in white robes, bearing clay ollas and ladles made of gourds.

The high priests already had the human sacrifices drugged and tied before the altar, in preparation for the dawn ceremonies, and they had been bowing before the altar all night, raising their voices in song and prayers.

Outside, lightning flashed in the distance and thunder rolled through the heavens. It was uncommon for Cahon to come and check on the high priests' work, but never before had the Brother to the Sun been forced to fight such demons— demons so powerful that they dared challenge the Great One himself!

Cahon walked among the sacrifices, checked to make sure that each had a prayer painted upon its forehead, checked the bonds. When he was done, Cahon himself went up to the altar and sat upon it, glaring down at his priests.

The priests began to mutter in fear as the acolytes, dressed all in white, came up at Cahon's back and put the ollas at his feet.

Cahon waved expansively, silently, at the ollas, bidding his priests to drink.

The high priest said, "O Brother to the Sun, what is this?"

But Cahon merely growled, as was his way, and bid him to drink.

The high priest approached the altar, walking on his knees, lifted a ladle and took a drink. The water in the bowl burned his throat like fire, made the eyes jiggle in his head.

He shouted jubilantly, "The Brother to the Sun has given us the heat of the sun, even in this, our darkest hour! Everyone partake!"

He himself raised a second dipper full, swallowed it down, and then staggered under its strange effect. Dozens of priests crawled forward to drink.

⊓⊓⊤⊓⊓

In his room, Cahon woke in great pain. A huge welt had raised on his forehead. He lay gagged and tied to a chair. He began immediately trying to work his hands free.

⊓⊓⊤⊓⊓

Behind the jaguar mask, Lotsa Smoke grinned a feral grin, while Pretty Rose and Bear Tail eagerly went to fill ollas with more firewater.

In minutes the priests in the temple were falling down drunk, and the high priest himself went out to the plaza and spread the cheer among Cahon's finest warriors.

Within half an hour, the warriors were not dancing around the fire so much as staggering. The drummers and flutists picked up their beat, playing a wild song that went howling over the city, reverberating from the ground.

Meanwhile, Lotsa Smoke and the squaws managed, barely, to get the jaguar god off its pedestal and wrapped in a heavy sack. Now they began dragging it downhill.

Dumphee crept near the front gate of the Mayan city and stood listening to the strange music coming from uphill. In the distance, lightning flashed and thunder rolled over the heavens.

But nearby the music was loud, the drums thrumming in a distinctive rock beat, the pipes playing loud and shrill. The Mayans danced around the bonfire in their huge pavilion. Dumphee thought he recognized the song. His friend Daniel LeBaron used to play it on the CD in his Ford Ranger. It sounded almost like the song "Iron Man," from Black Sabbath's *Paranoid* album.

Even worse, the warriors up there, dancing around in their shirts of mail with their battle-axes, looked like some demon zombie robots rising out of the earth. They twisted and gyrated like tormented things, laughing at one another's antics.

"Wow," Dumphee whispered under his breath. "How surreal!" Overhead, the clouds thickened. Gusts of wind pummeled the ground and sang through the cornfields. A storm was coming, a big one. Lightning flashed to the southwest.

Dumphee recognized drunkenness when he saw it. After all, fomenting drunkenness had been his family's primary occupation for nearly a hundred years.

His heart pounded in terror. They got the truck and the girls all right, he thought. And now they're drinking all of my fuel!

He had to put a stop to it!

—————

Cahon broke free of his bonds, grabbed his staff, and rushed out into the main part of the temple. He found his priests drunk and giggling on the floor, and someone had cut the ropes and freed all of his human sacrifices.

Worse, the golden jaguar god was gone, all of his precious sun metal taken!

Cahon snarled, a sound inspired by the jaguar he worshiped, and ran out to the front steps of the temple. His soldiers were all there dancing around like crazed madmen, laughing.

One of his generals staggered into the bonfire, and everyone pointed and began howling in laughter. He leapt out with a whoop, stood there laughing too, until he realized that his leggings were on fire. Then he hopped around on one foot, shouting, while everyone laughed harder.

Cahon cried out in rage: "You fools! We've been robbed! Find the demons who stole the jaguar god, or I'll sacrifice the whole lot of you at dawn!"

To his astonishment, the warriors all turned and looked at him with bleary eyes. They began pointing and laughing.

"Now!" Cahon shouted, pounding the base of his staff against the stone at the top of the landing. "Do it now!"

But his warriors merely mocked him.

He began running down the steps of the temple, intent on banging a few heads together.

—⊓⊓⊤⊓⊓—

Dumphee had Cahon in his sights. "Take this, you son of a jackass," he whispered, squeezing off a round.

Apparently after cooling for a while, the gun went back to its original program.

The giant red tongue appeared in front of Cahon, waggled and shouted the Russian version of "Nyah, nyah, nyah!" Though Dumphee now thought that it might have said *"Nyet, nyet, nyet."*

Cahon stared at it wide-eyed, tripped, and tumbled head-first down the steps of the temple.

He lay sprawled on the steps a moment, while his warriors laughed and hooted and pointed their fingers.

He jumped to his feet, snarling in rage like some animal.

Dumphee didn't give him time to recover.

He sent the fiery phoenix flying around Cahon's head, and suddenly the warriors stopped laughing.

215

Cahon stood, panting in his rage, teeth bared. He began looking around suspiciously, as if certain that Dumphee stood nearby.

He raised his own magical staff and began shouting to the heavens, trying to draw a curse on Dumphee.

So this is it, Dumphee thought. *Mano a mano*, god against god.

"Oh yeah?" Dumphee shouted. "Well, take that!"

The giant yellow armadillo did nothing for Cahon. He swatted at it with his staff, and Dumphee made a mental note to tell R & D that the armadillo really wasn't effective.

But Richard Nixon? Richard Nixon, now, *he* did the trick. When his hideous form loomed over Cahon belting out:

I see a bad moon arising.
I see trouble on the way!
I see earthquakes and lightnin'!

Cahon didn't even notice the fact that the image was making peace signs.

The old man froze, petrified with terror. His staff fell from his hands. Cahon trembled and crumpled to one knee on the steps of the temple.

His generals all began backing away, staggering and fleeing in terror, rolling down the steep sides of the mounds themselves.

⊤⊤⊤⊤

"Find the demons!" Cahon shouted. "Kill them all. Now!"

—ттгттг—

In the dark streets, Lotsa Smoke had finally gotten the jaguar downhill to the bottom of the mound and through most of the town. She was panting and sweating. But ahead the city gates were closed tight, and guards stood perched on the high towers.

As she stood there, listening to the screams of terror on the hill, she glanced back and saw the ghostly demon up there, singing in his paleface shorts.

"Oh, Dumphee come save us!" Pretty Rose chortled. "He so nice!"

Bear Tail laughed. "Yes, he like us plenty!"

"Come on," Lotsa Smoke said, urging the girls toward the city gates.

—ттгттг—

Just for the hell of it, Dumphee gave Cahon a dose of Stalin. As the fiery Russian cursed and waded among the damned forms of Elvis Presleys, a howl of alarm rose from the Mayans atop the mound.

To their great credit, proud warriors staggered forward with battle-axes and attacked the vaporous Elvises, while, suddenly, arrows and spears went arcing up into the giant form of Stalin himself.

Had the giant been real, he'd never have sat on a toilet comfortably again.

—⊓⊓⊔⊔—

As the ghostly demons were vanquished, Cahon shouted at his warriors: "Go now! Find them! Kill them all!"

The warriors turned and raced down the mound, shouting for the city guards to open the gates.

—⊓⊓⊔⊔—

As the guards threw the gates open, Lotsa Smoke and the squaws rushed out, lugging the heavy idol between them. The guards at the gates did not try to stop them. Obviously they were terrified of the demons.

But the hundreds of warriors racing down from the hill were flushed with enthusiasm at their recent defeat of Stalin. They screamed and shouted, waving their axes as they ran.

Arrows and spears plummeted all around the women, and even the guards atop the tower started taking potshots with fire arrows.

"Wagh," Bear Tail cried. "Help! Help! We gonna die!"

—⊓⊓⊔⊔—

Dumphee stood in the middle of the street and watched the girls run. A hundred warriors were on their tail, and more were rushing from the huts now, weapons in hand. He wished that he had the M-16.

Instead, he aimed at the girls' backs and fired his rifle.

The Statue of Liberty took form at the city gates, and immediately began swatting the nearest towers with her great wrecking ball. Everywhere through the city, from every wall, people cried out in horror. Now some Mayans leapt from the twenty-foot wall of the city to escape. The drunken warriors hurled their spears at her, ignoring the fleeing squaws.

Dumphee ran up to them. "Come on!" he shouted. "We got to go back in and get the truck!"

"Truck not there. Truck out here!" Lotsa Smoke shouted.

The squaws raced through a field of dry cornstalks a couple hundred yards, lugging some heavy bundles, and Dumphee followed up at the rear.

When he reached the truck, he was astonished to find it all loaded and intact.

The squaws picked up their heavy sacks, heaved them into the back of the truck, and began laughing in relief.

"Oh, you come save us!" Lotsa Smoke yelled in delight. "You come save us!"

"Him plenty worried!" Bear Tail agreed.

Pretty Rose jumped up and down. "He like us! Chiefy want us!"

Soon, the squaws were on him, kissing him and laughing, pressing against him, and Dumphee had never felt so heroic.

"Ladies, let's get out of here," Dumphee whispered.

"Wait!" Lotsa Smoke shouted. "We have present!"

She took one of the heavy bags she'd carried from the temple, dumped it into the back of the truck, and flipped on the overhead light. Gold was everywhere—spoons, necklaces, bracelets, idols.

Then she opened a second bag, showed him the kneeling jaguar, and set it up before Dumphee—the emeralds in its golden eyes gleaming, its ruby lips smiling. Little crusts of diamonds were set in the cat's teeth. Dumphee stared at the magnificent idol in awe.

"This for you, Chiefy," Lotsa Smoke said. "You great hero. This present for you!"

Dumphee considered the idol. He felt downcast. He hadn't really saved the girls. He'd helped them rob the Mayans.

And immediately he saw that his own small part in this affair was assuming great proportions. Someday, white men would come to this country and the Mayans would mistake them for gods. The return of the great white god Quetzalcoatl. There were hundreds of tales of a white-skinned, blond-haired, blue-eyed man who had been a god come down from the sky. Legends said he had the power of the sun and fire.

Dumphee scratched at the sandy blond beard that had been growing on his face for the past few weeks and considered his own bright blue eyes.

"Oh, shit," he realized. "I'm in the history books now no matter what I do."

Because he'd come here, he had affected the space-time continuum in some way. He'd become the seed of a legend, a legend that would lead future Mayans to worship and succumb to the conquistadors, leading to the downfall of a whole civilization.

What to do? What to do? he wondered. He should be mad at the girls for stealing from the Mayans. At the same time, those same Mayans had come to take them as human sacrifices just a few hours ago. Maybe they did owe the squaws something.

"Aw, to hell with 'em," he said. "Thank you."

Lotsa Smoke hopped behind the wheel of the ATV, started the engine, and sent the vehicle wheeling toward the road that led to the Mayan city.

When she got out of the cornfield, she flipped on the headlights and pointed them toward the city gates.

A huge war party had gathered there, and Cahon was screaming at his chiefs, trying to urge them to come out into the night and attack the truck.

Lotsa Smoke honked the air horn, scaring some back into the city, and as she halted for a moment, Bear Tail fired an anti-aircraft missile into the city walls, just to get Cahon's attention.

The old man stood there for a moment glaring, panting. He looked at the vast hole in the city wall, and even from a distance, Lotsa Smoke could see that he was frightened, defeated.

Lotsa Smoke got out, made a warning gesture, and gave one last message to Cahon.

—————

As they drove from the Mayan city and let the ATV ford the Mississippi, Lotsa Smoke broke out a couple of cigars they'd captured from the French, and Dumphee did indulge.

The water carried them downstream faster than the ATV crossed the river, and Dumphee remembered dully that Quetzalcoatl, too, was supposed to have last been seen sailing across the great waters.

Well, he decided, the Mississippi went into the ocean, and as far as the Mayans knew, that was where he was headed.

Still, something bothered him. Legend said that before Quetzalcoatl had departed from his people, he had promised to return.

He asked Lotsa Smoke, "Just before we left, you signed something to Cahon. What did you say?"

Wearing gold bangles on her wrists and chains around her neck, she grinned at Dumphee. "I not want them to follow. I tell them, you be back!"

CHAPTER 27

Major Slice had almost put Dumphee out of mind when he got a phone call on a secure line.

"Major Slice, this is Captain Jones. We spoke a few weeks ago regarding the Dumphee case."

Slice considered the name. The voice he recognized, but not the name. "Wait a minute. You're the fellow from the Pentagon, right? Top-Secret Security stuff?"

"Yes," the voice answered.

"I thought you said your name was Smith?"

"Whatever," the voice answered. "Smith, Jones, Captain, General. It doesn't really matter now, does it, sir?"

Slice got a very unsettled feeling in his stomach.

"Okay, so what have you got for me?"

"I've been doing some research on time-anomalous arti-facts. It's a rather painstaking process, since we don't have the catalogs computerized yet."

"Okay, okay," Slice said. "So what the hell does that have to do with Dumphee?"

"Well, it's a long shot, but I've been trying to connect the dots—you know, figure out what route he might have fol-lowed, see if I can track him anywhere."

"And?"

"And," the voice answered, "I had some luck. In the Cahokia Mounds in southern Illinois, where a major Mayan city once stood, I found a catalog mention of an ancient Mohawk tomahawk that was kept in the temple."

"What's that have to do with Dumphee?"

"Well, carbon-dating shows that the tomahawk is old—about a thousand years older than any other Mohawk artifact ever found.

"Of course, I reasoned that it could have been buried on the spot, but we took the trouble of sending a research team back for some more digging. We found small chunks of metal outside the compound—super-heated fragments. It looked like slag or something, and no one had bothered to analyze it before. But I did. It seems the mixture was too modern—the slag came from a steel rocket with a titanium armor-piercing tip. The steel composition matches that produced from a modern steel mill in Kazakhstan."

"So, you're telling me that Dumphee blew the hell out of a bunch of Mayans?" Slice asked, tapping his pen against his desk. He looked out the window. It was high summer in Denver, and the compound was hot. Steam rose from the tarmac outside his office after the morning's rain.

"Precisely, Major."

"Well," Slice said, "I know we've never officially declared war against the Mayans or anything, but from what I know of them, all I can say is, bully for Private Dumphee."

"My sentiments exactly," the voice answered.

Slice wondered what the fellow might be leading up to.

"So, by looking at Dumphee's line of travel," Jones said, "I've deduced that he was heading for Denver when last seen."

"How can you deduce that?"

"The legend of Quetzalcoatl," the voice answered. "The god Quetzalcoatl was a man who spoke an unknown tongue. He had blond hair and blue eyes, just like our Dumphee, and he was last seen in a strange ship, heading across the water. We'd always assumed from legends that he was in the Pacific Ocean, but if he'd driven west over the Mississippi, then Dumphee would have been heading toward Denver, still.

"Dumphee *is* the Mayan god Quetzalcoatl."

Slice licked his lips. "Hmmm," he said. "Well, I kind of figured that if Dumphee ever made it back, maybe I'd give him a promotion—but a *god*? Hell, how can I beat that?

"Tell me, did these Mayans mention anything about him disappearing into a cloud—any color of cloud, maybe an ecru-colored cloud? Or even a dusky magenta?"

225

"No, they didn't," Jones answered.

"Well," Slice said, "that's a shame."

After a long pause, Jones said, "You will of course notify me the moment that Dumphee arrives."

"What do you mean?" Slice said. "He's already months overdue."

"Perhaps," Jones said. "But I don't think it's a matter of *if* he arrives, but *when* . . ."

"All right, then," Slice said. "When—if—he arrives, I'll notify you first thing."

"No," Jones said. "You will arrest him and put him in solitary confinement, until we can determine the extent to which he suffers from temporal contamination."

"Tempor-uh what?"

"*Temporal contamination:* Usually this refers to contamination of beliefs, concepts or philosophy due to exposure to future timelines. But it can also refer to physical contamination from archaic or futuristic disease-causing organisms or parasites."

"Futuristic disease-causing organisms?"

"Drink the water in Mexico, and you'll come home with dysentery," Smith or Jones or whatever-his-name said in a matter-of-fact tone. "But if you drink the water in 2441, you'll *wish* you had something as quaint as dysentery. So when Dumphee arrives, I want him jailed and in isolation."

"But . . . on what charge?" Slice asked.

"Time travel is illegal," Jones said firmly.

"But . . . I've never heard of any laws against it!" Slice objected.

"Oh!" Jones said, as if in surprise. Then he promised in a deadly tone, "But there *will* be. There will be."

He quietly dropped the receiver.

CHAPTER 28

Ten days after leaving the Mayan temple, Dumphee found himself rolling across the desert into Colorado at slow speed. The weight of all the gold and supplies slowed the ATV and depleted the fuel reserves faster than expected.

Yet the ride through Missouri and Kansas had been pleasant. There were plenty of buffalo and antelope on the plains, and surprisingly few Mayans, and the going was steady. Fifteen miles per hour was the average speed under good conditions. Sometimes they slowed to five.

Now, as they drove, the squaws were all dressed in gold—gold bracelets, gold headbands and necklaces, golden Mayan earrings used as buttons.

Yet the squaws were just as happy to have cigars and fire-water as they were to have gold. Food was plentiful.

Life seemed good.

"Oh, we count plenty coup!" Bear Tail said one evening around the campfire as she fingered her new golden bracelets.

"That's right, you're one hell of a Rambo," Dumphee laughed.

"Mohawk!" Bear Tail said. "I Mohawk!"

"Nope," Dumphee said, "I've decided that you're a Rambo. That's a title of heap big honor where I come from. Very great brave."

"Oh!" Bear Tail smiled and tried to look stern at the same time.

"I Rambo, too?" Lotsa Smoke asked. She explained, "I daughter of heap big brave."

"Nope, you're not a Rambo, I'm afraid. You're too pretty. Where I come from, you're called a *ten*."

"Oh," Lotsa Smoke said, mystified. "That good?"

"That's very good," Dumphee said.

Lotsa Smoke smiled proudly.

"What I?" Pretty Rose asked.

"You? You're a *goofball*."

"*Goof* . . . ball?" Pretty Rose asked.

"Yeah," Dumphee said, "like a *football*, but without so many feet."

Pretty Rose gave him a questioning scowl.

The next afternoon, another autumn storm thundered in. Lightning arced across the sky, and the dust blew up, just as hail and rain began to pummel the ATV. In a few moments, Lotsa Smoke stuck her head into the window from the back.

"Wagh, me getting wet!" she grumbled.

Dumphee shook his head. "Not much we can do about it," he answered. The sabertooths had slashed the canopy of the truck, so the squaws had patched it with buckskins. Now the wind and the storm seemed determined to undo their labor.

"No place sleep back here," she grumbled. Sleeping space was at a premium, what with all the gold. "Must find shelter."

Dumphee shook his head. "I don't think there's much shelter around here. It might be better to just keep on driving."

"I saw mountain ahead, just before hail fall. Maybe we go there," Lotsa Smoke said.

It had been a lonely pinnacle of rock with a broad base. Dumphee felt sure he'd seen it before in some old western movie. Or maybe those lonely pinnacles were everywhere out here.

"I don't know," Dumphee answered. "I don't think it will offer much shelter."

Lightning slashed across the sky, shooting from horizon to horizon.

"Please?" Lotsa Smoke said. "I scared." She leaned her head into the front of the ATV and nibbled on his ear.

Dumphee's heart raced. "I don't know."

"We find shelter," Lotsa Smoke argued. "You come back, keep me warm. I scared."

She reached through the window, put her hand beneath his shirt and stroked the hairs of his chest.

"I don't know," Dumphee shook his head. "You girls got me all worn out."

"Oh, brave chief, very great," Lotsa Smoke said. "No can get worn out."

Pretty Rose clutched his shoulder, whispering, "Please find safe place. I scared too! Oh, very scared!" She stretched forward and kissed him passionately on the lips.

Dumphee absolutely hated it when these women got each other feeling passionate.

"All right," he said. "I'll try to find us some shelter. But I am not sleeping with you women! Honestly, you remind me of a bunch of wildcats!"

He turned the wheel of the ATV and headed for the lee of that mountain.

He'd not gone far when the headlights showed a sudden drop in his path—a gully with steep sides, some sixty feet deep. The ATV couldn't negotiate that incline. Dumphee would have to go around.

He turned into a screen of sagebrush, tall as a man, with a few twisted junipers thrown in, and picked a narrow spot to push through. Lightning flashed, blinding him.

Thunder snarled and rolled across the plain. Dumphee listened for a moment, but the rumbling continued, growing louder.

Dumphee stopped the ATV.

"What that?" Bear Tail asked.

Dumphee listened. The ATV trembled in concert with the distant rumbling.

"That's not thunder . . ." Dumphee said. He wiped some steam off his window and looked out over the hill. Lightning flashed, and in that flash he saw a dark roiling tide of flesh, light dancing upon thousands of curved horns, all heading right toward him. He shouted, "Buffalo stampede!"

He hit the gas, slued right through the junipers.

Suddenly a chasm opened in front of him, a little spur from a narrow canyon. He slammed the brakes, but the vehicle couldn't stop, not with so much gold in it.

The truck slid into the chasm. It took all of Dumphee's control to keep from crashing into the rocks at the bottom of the gully. He twisted right and left to miss the rocks, then steered toward a juniper, spinning out of control.

"Wagh!" Lotsa Smoke shouted as a peach-colored fog enveloped the truck.

CHAPTER 29

As the mist swallowed them, Dumphee cringed.

The ATV rolled to its side. In the back Bear Tail screamed as gold and ivory all shifted. The time machine heaved almost clean out of the truck, smashing into the top of the canopy.

In his mind's eye, Dumphee saw those *Do Not Jolt* signs on the back of that box.

As the vehicle settled on its side, Dumphee heard air hiss from tires. He looked out through a peach-colored haze at the trunk of a giant fern tree, nearly as wide as the ATV itself. He gripped the seat as gold settled in the back of the truck.

He listened to the sounds of a deep forest all around—the whirring of insects and the peeping of frogs. A giant dragonfly with a wingspan of two feet whipped past, grabbing a mosquito the size of a sparrow right out of the air.

Distantly, bellows and cries arose from giant animals. Sounds no man had ever heard.

"Oh, shit," he wanted to say. But he'd read somewhere that those were the most common words people said just before they died. He didn't want to jinx himself.

Lotsa Smoke climbed out of the cab on the passenger's side, looked around at the fern trees, then kicked a tire. "Oh, blast," she said. "Tire heap plenty dead."

CHAPTER 30

A quick inspection of the ATV showed that Dumphee had flattened two tires that had run over some piece of bone with lots of wicked spikes. He'd have to unload the truck, tilt it right, then change and patch the tires before loading it up again.

Unloading the truck was easy, but Dumphee didn't want to turn his back—on anything.

He kept twisting, watching over his shoulder. He put all three squaws on guard with heavy weapons, and refused to let them help repair the truck. They were on an unprotected rise where a sea of fern trees blew in a lonely wind. The air smelled fetid and muddy; distant smoke from a volcano dirtied the air and left it smelling sulfuric.

Lotsa Smoke kept gazing at that volcano expectantly. "We near Denver now?" she asked. "This fire mountain that makes firewater?"

"We're close," he admitted. Just then the ground trembled, shaking beneath his feet as from a mild earthquake.

"Hmmm . . ." Pretty Rose ventured. "Me hear buffalo stampede."

The volcano flared, spraying ash and fire into the air.

"Not a stampede," Dumphee said.

"Manitou heap mad," Lotsa Smoke said. "You not sleep with squaws."

"I don't think Manitou has anything to do with it," Dumphee said.

A flock of pterodactyls with thirty-foot wingspans soared above the trees. They made no sound, just glided over like shadows. Bear Tail shot a round into the air.

"Manitou angry," Lotsa Smoke affirmed. "He mad you give firewater to squaws."

"Maybe you convert to Christian again," Dumphee said. "At least the Christian God doesn't punish you until you're dead."

"No," Pretty Rose grumbled. "Christian God not mean enough to bring people here with giant birds. This Manitou work."

"Yeah," Dumphee said. "Maybe you're right."

Signs of dinosaurs were everywhere—huge, three-toed dinosaur tracks were etched deep into the forest floor. Bones were strewn about from some past meal. An enormous tree canted sideways where a dinosaur had leaned against it to scratch.

Dumphee worked with shaking hands to gently unload the time machine and gold from the ATV. When the ATV was empty, he had the women help him get logs and use them as levers until he propped the truck upright. Then he patched the tires and reloaded the vehicle.

When he finished, he stared longingly at the time machine. All right, he considered. Whenever we've dropped, and the weight of that thing has pressed down, we've gone back in time. This last fall was the biggest, and we went back furthest.

But when I kicked the machine from the bottom, exerting pressure upward, we went forward in time.

It seemed only obvious that if he learned to kick it just right—give it the perfect combination of taps up or down or forward or backward—he could sort of control the machine, move it to the time he wanted.

Maybe.

But maybe was dangerous as hell.

The thing was, right now they were safe. But what if he gave the thing a little kick, and it put him right in the middle of a dinosaur stampede? Or took him back to the beginning of the world? He vaguely remembered from a science class that before the world formed, there was only propane or some damned poisonous gas in the atmosphere. Or what if it took him to the end of time, when the sun was just a cold cinder in the sky? He'd freeze to death before he had time to blink.

He opened the box to the time machine; the squaws drew near.

"What Chiefy do?" Lotsa Smoke asked, gazing at the orb of light within the container.

"Ladies, we've got a problem. We're back here in the dinosaur age, and I don't think we want to be here. I'm sort of tempted to just give this time machine a good hard whack and see where it takes us, but it's a gamble. We could end up in an ocean, or in the middle of a range fire, or find ourselves trampled by grumpalumps." He used the squaw's word, *grumpalumps*, for mastodons.

At the mention of grumpalumps, Pretty Rose drew back in fear.

"But there's worse things than grumpalumps here," Dumphee said.

"What kind things?" Pretty Rose asked, her voice soft and frightened. She glanced back up at the sky for sign of more pterodactyls.

"I don't know for sure. Probably *Tyrannosaurus rexes*." Dumphee had to think a moment. What was the plural of *Tyrannosaurus rex*, anyway? It was a mouthful to say. "They're big critters." But how big? he wondered. "Big enough to grab a grumpalump by the scruff of the neck and eat him for lunch, I think."

For once, Lotsa Smoke didn't look askance at Dumphee and accuse him of lying. The giant birds she'd seen had convinced her.

"So I think that maybe it's time for us to make a decision," Dumphee said.

"What decide?" Lotsa Smoke asked.

"I think I ought to sort of experiment. But in doing so, I'd be risking all of our lives.

"But I won't risk your lives without your permission. I think I ought to just start knocking this time machine around to see if we can get a little closer to our own time zone. I can't promise to get you ladies back to your own place and time, but I might get you close."

"Get back to our time? What you do then?" Bear Tail asked.

"I'll give you as much gold as you want, and let you make your own way." Dumphee stared at each squaw to see how she took the news. He was offering them their freedom—or death.

"I want come with you!" Pretty Rose cried. "You my husband."

Dumphee shook his head. "Not *when* I come from. There, a man only has one wife. You're good squaws, but I'm not sure you'd ever learn to fit in."

"You no like us?" Lotsa Smoke asked, her face getting hard and angry.

"It isn't that," Dumphee said. "It's just, where I come from, everything is so different. You'd have to get a job, and explain

241

to the government where you came from, and learn how to drive—"

"I drive," Lotsa Smoke said.

Dumphee shook his head. "It's learning to read and write—"

"I read whole Bible at mission school," Lotsa Smoke said. "I read good. I remember . . .

> The Lord is my shepherd,
> I shall not want—

"I read Malory and Shakespeare," Pretty Rose said. "I smarter than you."

"You don't understand," Dumphee said. "That's not good enough. You wouldn't fit in. You're not civilized. . . ."

"I stay here, then," Pretty Rose said with a tone of finality.

"What?" Dumphee asked astonished. "You can't do that!"

"No go back to own time. I go back, maybe Seneca or Frenchie kill me. That no good."

"Ughhh," Lotsa Smoke nodded in agreement, as if seeing that Pretty Rose spoke wisely. She crouched down on the ground, staring thoughtfully at a dinosaur track. "No go back to Mayan time, either. We all get killed, sure."

"Ugh," Bear Tail agreed, cradling her antitank gun close against her chest. "We find some good tribe here, live with them."

"There isn't any good tribe here," Dumphee said. "There are *no* people here. No people anywhere in the world. There's only dinosaur monsters, like those saber-toothed lions, only worse!"

"Sabertooth, Seneca, Mayan, paleface, dinosaur—" Pretty Rose said, shaking her head. "All same to me. I no belong anywhere."

"God . . ." Dumphee breathed, because he knew she was right. He couldn't save her. He couldn't take her back to her own time. He didn't have enough fuel to get back to Pittsburgh. Maybe if he could get her back, he could take her sometime safe, take her back to live as her grandparents had lived.

But then what would happen? She'd know the future, know what the white men would bring, and she'd fight it. The whole course of history might be altered. And what would it gain her, personally?

He had no idea how long people lived in America in her day. What was the average life expectancy. Thirty years? The girl would most likely die from illness or in childbirth. No, he needed to get her someplace where she could have good medical attention. But if he brought them into his own time, he wouldn't be able to leave them on their own, where they could be taken advantage of. They'd end up in prison or on the streets, or maybe trying to live off the land. No, he'd have to take care of them, and treat them as they wanted to be treated, as true wives.

At long last, he asked, "What—what can I do? What is it you want?"

Lotsa Smoke planted the butt of her rifle on the ground, looked up into the sky. "I want take gold, buy good land for Indian. Big valleys, where deer and buffalo heap plenty. I want place where nice river, with lots of berries and yams. I want raise children in lodge, in peace. Not always be afraid."

Pretty Rose began to sniffle, and Bear Tail grunted her agreement. "Yes. Good dream. No be afraid."

Yet she wanted more. "You say we no civilize enough," Pretty Rose continued. "No can take us your home. It no good for us. Mayans, they got civilize, but it no good for us. French got civilize, but it no good.

"I say, civilize no good. Maybe I no want be civilize. I want live where people good to each other. No hurt each other. You take us there."

Dumphee considered. He didn't know of any place quite like what Pretty Rose wanted. He hadn't seen a civilization where she would be allowed to live free and happy. Maybe it was there, somewhere in the future, but he hadn't seen the future yet.

Nope, maybe there wasn't even such a thing as the kind of civilization that Pretty Rose wanted.

In which case, Pretty Rose was right: they might all just as well live with the sabertooths as in some godforsaken place like New York City.

Dumphee considered his world. West Virginia didn't look too bad. The best of lands, the best of times, a place that his ancestors had never quite dreamed of. Maybe back in the early seventies, when the hippies were infiltrating the mountains and people were a little more open-minded, one man living with three squaws might not have raised too many eyebrows.

His mom and dad had grown up in that time. The only thing that had seemed oppressive about the sixties had been the tail end of Vietnam and the Cold War, and Dumphee knew now how those would end.

With all the gold they had in the back of the ATV, they could buy half of West Virginia, if they wanted. It really wasn't difficult to imagine himself living happily with the squaws. They could hire servants to care for the house and run the vacuum cleaners. They could hire chauffeurs and cooks. The squaws wouldn't need to learn that much.

Hell, with enough money, anything was possible.

"All right, then," Dumphee said. "If you girls will have me, then I'll take you to my time, if I can get us there alive. And I promise: you'll like it. You can learn to drive cars, and live in a house that never gets cold. You can take baths in warm water every day. We have doctors there who will make sure that you live to a good old age, and you'll never be hungry. I think you'll like it."

"And good people? You got good people there?" Pretty Rose asked.

"Most of 'em," Dumphee said, "though there's always a few wormy apples in every barrel. And we'll be rich enough so that those who aren't nice will have to live in unholy terror of us."

Dumphee got kind of choked up as he talked. He was asking them to marry him and be his wives, though some folks might frown on that. Only problem was, as far as the squaws were concerned, they already *were* his wives.

"What we do for fun there?" Lotsa Smoke asked.

"I'll fly you to Disney World, to ride on the rides," Dumphee said. "That will be fun."

"Disney World? Whole other world?" Lotsa Smoke cocked her brow with interest.

"Close enough," Dumphee said.

"Sound good," Bear Tail agreed. "We put mastodon teeth over fireplace, make rug of sabertooth skin. Show everyone how you great warrior."

"We make cups of gold, like Holy Father had for sacrament!" Pretty Rose added.

"Then we're all agreed?" Dumphee said. "We should try to go back?"

Out over the forest, a tremendous roar issued—some huge beast nearby. The sun slanted through the fern trees. It would be dark soon. The squaws all looked off toward the sound.

Pretty Rose's face was frightened.

"Let's get out of here," Dumphee said. He studied the time machine, trying to decide just how to nudge it. He'd have to give it a pretty good wallop to move them very far.

Dumphee made as if to hit the time machine, knowing that it might be his last act.

Pretty Rose grabbed his arm and shouted, "Wait!"

"Yeah?" Dumphee asked. "What for?"

"We maybe all die if you hit time machine, right?" she asked.

"There's a chance," Dumphee said.

"Me want see dinosaurs first," Pretty Rose pleaded.

"Me want *kill* dinosaurs," Bear Tail begged, patting her gun. "Heap big medicine. Put teeth on mantel. Let people know, we mighty brave! We brave squaws!"

"Ughhh," Lotsa Smoke said, "Good idea!"

Dumphee licked his lips, glanced from squaw to squaw, and saw Pretty Rose give a little twisted smile. They all wanted to go into the future, but none of them really wanted to risk dying right this minute.

And because they were from a culture that honored people for mad acts of daring, they were trying to put a brave face on it.

Somehow, Dumphee found himself warming to the idea, too. After all, if he was going to die in thirty seconds, wouldn't it be sad if he did so without ever seeing a dinosaur? When would he get another chance?

Back when he was a kid, his uncle Ned would take him up in the mountains in his old red Ford pickup, driving over the gravel roads until the dogs in the back caught scent of a bear and began to bay. At age twelve, Dumphee had imagined that he was brave to go chasing off through those woods after a bear. It was, after all, a big wild animal, and he was just a kid with a gun.

But the first time his uncle ever treed a sow and her cubs, then shot her down from the tree, Dumphee had learned the truth: hunting bears with dogs was a coward's act. Those bears weren't anywhere as big and frightening as they looked on television. There was no honor to it.

But a *dinosaur?* A *Tyrannosaurus rex!* And no dogs to tree it. Hell, he'd have to get its head stuffed and mounted over the fireplace! Dumphee began to grin maniacally.

Then he got to thinking about those pterodactyls, and imagined a nice big one with its wings spread wide and its head looking up, sort of the way a mallard would be prepared for the wall.

In fact, he imagined that if he could get this time machine working right, he might even go find his uncle Ned and show him what real big-game hunting was like!

And Dumphee was willing to bet that there would be plenty of folks willing to pay good money to hunt dinosaurs—folks like Teddy Roosevelt and Ernest Hemingway and other short millionaires who couldn't think of a better way to prove their manhood.

Dumphee wondered if Hitler or Napoleon had ever liked to hunt. If so, he might even be able to bring them here and arrange a little accident.

He imagined Hitler drawing down on a charging T-rex and dropping the hammer on his big gun, only to have it go *clink!*

Dumphee would have filed down the firing pin, of course.

But no, that seemed too sanitary an ending for a man like Hitler.

"Well," Dumphee said, "if we're going to go hunt us some dinosaurs, I guess we'd best get going."

CHAPTER 31

Dumphee sat on the roof of the ATV, antitank rifle in hand, while Lotsa Smoke drove. His legs dangled down over the windshield, so that Lotsa Smoke peeked out from between his legs.

The squaws had gotten out his CD player and had turned up Bill Monroe playing "Foggy Mountain Breakdown."

He could see dinosaur tracks just ahead. He couldn't be sure, but he thought they might be from a *Tyrannosaurus rex*. They were huge, three-toed, and the monster had to be walking twelve or fifteen feet to a pace.

Dumphee had a pretty good view of the forest ahead. Off to his right, an ankylosaur ambled through the woods, bearing several tons of bone plating on its heavy frame. When it saw the truck, it hissed and backed away, the heavy armored clubs on its tail swinging like a mace.

"That tyrosaurex?" Bear Tail asked.

"Nah," Dumphee said. In the past hour, the girls had asked him about a number of dinosaurs, and he'd answered "Nah," each time. He wasn't sure, but he thought he might have discovered a few new species—at least there were varieties that he'd never encountered in his plastic bags as a kid.

Up ahead, the ground was nearly covered in wispy fog. He could see pools of hot water everywhere. "Bear to the left!" Dumphee said, aiming her between the pools.

Lotsa Smoke flipped on her headlights, skirting the edge of the hot springs. Boiling mud bubbled in mud pots or came sputtering from the ground. Ahead, water suddenly geysered up out of a pool and came raining down on the truck.

Dumphee whooped and yelped and leapt down. That water was hot! He jumped into the cab of the truck while Lotsa Smoke searched for the windshield wiper button.

She got the wipers working while Dumphee peeled off his hot wet clothes. He said, "Man, now I know how a pig feels in a scalding pot!"

He got his shirt off when Bear Tail asked, "That *Tyrannosaurus rex?*"

"Where?" Dumphee shouted, looking up at the windshield, just as Lotsa Smoke got the wipers working.

The wiper blades slashed through the water to reveal a huge T-rex, its teeth dripping saliva, staring down through the windshield not two yards from the front bumper.

"Aaagh!" Dumphee cried. His heart began hammering in his chest, and he suddenly had to pee more badly than he'd ever had to in his life.

Bear Tail reached past him and pushed open the door. "You go shoot 'em."

Dumphee fumbled to pull the door closed, fighting against Bear Tail.

"Yay, Chiefy!" Pretty Rose encouraged him. "Him heap brave."

"I'm not brave!" Dumphee shouted, finally getting the door closed.

When he looked up again, the T-rex was gone. A cloud of spray and mist still hung in the air. He looked all around, then asked, "Where did it go?"

"That way!" Lotsa Smoke said, jutting her chin toward the mist.

Bear Tail got the door open again. She said, "Go get 'em!"

"Yeah," Lotsa Smoke said. "We wait here!"

Dumphee reached to pull the door closed. His hand was shaking so badly, he had the irrational thought that there must be another earthquake somewhere, causing it.

He gripped his antitank rifle and gritted his teeth. He inspected the chamber to make sure that one of the huge shells was inside, then checked the safety and flipped it off.

He climbed out of the truck on rubbery legs, just as hot water geysered up a hundred yards ahead. The water just kept going up and up, forming something of a mushroom cloud overhead, and Dumphee watched it for a long minute in wonder. He'd seen pictures of Old Faithful back in Yellowstone, but he'd never seen anything like this.

Then the warm rain came down, drenching him from head to foot.

He stared ahead, tried to peer through the fog. He couldn't see a thing.

He set off. The mud squished beneath his boots, at least six inches deep. It sucked off one boot. He found the T-rex tracks, hunched low and made off through the mist. After he'd gone forty yards, he looked back through the fog, but couldn't see a thing.

Ahead he heard a low growl, deep and thunderous, maybe a hundred yards away. Then the T-rex snorted and loped to the west on heavy feet, pounding the ground with each step.

Dumphee scrabbled along, hunched low. He followed the T-rex tracks for a hundred yards, and saw where it had loped over a small hill into the thick fern trees.

He moves too fast, Dumphee realized. I'll never be able to catch him.

Just then the horn of the ATV belched, the squaws screamed, and he heard the vehicle's engine roar.

The ATV came rushing toward him, its headlights bouncing as it rolled through the mud, and the squaws shouted, "Dumphee! Dumphee!"

The ATV pulled up beside him. Dumphee jumped in.

All the squaws were shouting at once. "Heap big tyrosaur!" "Circle around behind!"

Lotsa Smoke punched the gas. The ATV rolled over the mud, dove into a pool of hot water, and the tires began to spin.

Behind the truck, in the fog, Dumphee heard an angry roar. Lotsa Smoke punched the gas harder, and the tires spun in the water.

"Get us out of here, before that geyser blows again!" Dumphee shouted.

Bear Tail turned and climbed through the curtain, into the back of the truck, and Dumphee vaulted out behind her. Through the mist came the *Tyrannosaurus rex* racing up to the edge of the hot water, where it lashed its tail and stuck in one dainty foot. The monster rolled its eyes and stuck out its tongue.

Dumphee fumbled with his gun. Bear Tail raised the barrel, pointing toward the *Tyrannosaurus rex.* "Shoot! Shoot now!" she urged.

Dumphee was shaking terribly. He pulled the trigger.

The gun went *click!*

"Dud!" Dumphee yelled, fumbling with his weapon. He opened the chamber, flipped out the dud shell, then realized that the gun didn't have another round in the magazine.

"Reload!" Dumphee shouted, looking around for ammunition.

Bear Tail glanced down at the boxes and crates full of experimental weapons, threw one aside. Beneath it was a tomahawk. She grabbed it, eyed the *Tyrannosaurus rex* critically, then said, "That no good!" and tossed it from the truck.

Dumphee knocked over a case of experimental weapons, some kind of flares or something. "Damn these stupid weapons!" he cried.

The *Tyrannosaurus rex* had tested the water, and now came wading out toward them.

The wheels of the ATV spun madly, exhaust poured from the back of the vehicle, but the T-rex was gaining.

Dumphee threw down his weapon and grabbed an M-16. The T-rex gaped its jaws. Its whole form filled up the back of the truck. Its teeth were as long as daggers and its breath smelled like a slaughterhouse. It had gotten up to its chest, and now it lowered its head and splashed in like a giant crocodile.

Water began to bubble all around the ATV—huge roiling bubbles that hissed steam.

"Lotsa Smoke, get us out of here!" Dumphee shouted.

But the ATV was already hitting its peak speed in water— two and a half miles per hour.

Dumphee pulled the trigger of the M-16. Nothing. He looked down, the safety was on.

Suddenly there was a huge rumbling sound and the ATV leaned precariously. The T-rex opened its eyes wide in terror and turned to swim back for shore.

The geyser blew, throwing the truck up into the air. Dumphee stared in surprise as the T-rex went hurtling above them. The whole truck tipped sideways as if it would flip into the geyser, and the gold shifted.

Dumphee turned back toward the time machine, just as Bear Tail gave it a boot.

No soccer player had ever kicked a ball with more gusto.

CHAPTER 32

The truck came out in daylight. A sunny day. The fern trees were gone, along with the geysers and volcanoes and dinosaurs. Instead, the land was a desert again, full of juniper and sagebrush.

Dumphee found himself tangled with Bear Tail and the weapons. He fought free of her and stared out the back of the truck.

He'd traveled ahead through time. His mouth felt dry with excitement. The ATV sat steaming and dripping in the morning sun.

The engine had died, so Lotsa Smoke fired it and drove up a small rise.

Dumphee did not dare to speak his wildest hopes.

They reached the top of the hill. Dumphee climbed out to the top of the truck and looked around.

Across the prairie, he saw it: a building. A simple building. A train station—with a water tower and a supply of logs. And there were phone wires strung beside the track.

In wonder, he stared. Distantly, he heard a train whistle. A puff of white smoke formed on the horizon.

"Steam-powered train," he whispered. "Maybe early nineteen hundreds. Maybe as late as 1940."

He was close to home. It felt good. I could live in this time, he thought. It wouldn't be home, but it would be close.

He banged on the top of the truck. "That-a-way!" he shouted. Lotsa Smoke hit the gas and drove toward the station. As they drew near, he saw that one side of the train station was scorched. It had taken fire not too long back.

There were two tracks ahead. One drove straight through. A parallel spur went to the water tower. By the water tower were dozens of spare railroad ties and a huge pile of cut firewood.

"Dang," Dumphee said when he saw the firewood. "This isn't going to be a real train. This is old stuff." He revised his estimate backward a few years. Definitely earlier than the forties.

He stopped the ATV and looked at the wires overhead. He could make a phone call. Perhaps he could turn this experimental weaponry over to the U.S. Army. That way, he would discharge his duty and be quit of it.

Dumphee parked under the water tower to wait for the train. In a few minutes it could be seen in the distance, fifty cars in all.

The squaws stared at the train in varying degrees of astonishment. "What that? What?" Pretty Rose shouted.

"It huge snake!" Lotsa Smoke said. "It breathe fire and scream like giant owl."

"That, dear ladies," Dumphee said, "is a steam-powered locomotive. It's like our ATV here, only not so fancy. It carries people inside."

He got out of the ATV to wait beside the train tracks with the squaws. Soon it pulled up to the water tank, with steam brakes whistling and the crash of couplings. The squaws watched.

The engineer, an old fellow with a thick beard and a sweaty bald head, eyed the squaws suspiciously as he pulled in. Up on the firebox, a muscular young man pulled out a rifle and brandished it.

As the train ground to a stop, the engineer leered at Dumphee. "Them yer squaws, Mister?"

Dumphee nodded.

"Well, so long as you keep 'em in line."

He shouted to the passenger cars behind.

"You can git on out, folks. Ya'll can stretch yer laigs a bit, whilst me an' the boys load some wood."

A bunch of eastern dudes with beaver-skin hats and vested suits all got down from the train, along with a few ladies with hoop skirts and parasols. After so long away from modern society, Dumphee thought that these painted folks looked as odd as clowns in a circus. Several men made big shows of consulting their gold watches.

The brakeman, a sooty little fellow, looked up to the engineer. "I don't like this place," he whispered. "I sure hope the Cheyenne Special gets here on time. Then we can highball it on out of here."

The engineer seemed to think a moment, then yelled at the passengers who were de-training. "Don't none of you folks git yerselfs lost. When I yell 'All aboard,' ya all jump aboard, lickety-split like. Or I'll leave ya behind to git scalped."

Dumphee stared at the engineer. "Scalped?"

"Dang right, scalped. Ten days ago, the Arapaho lit fire to this place. They scalped the station agent and the telegrapher. Filthy warhoops!"

Dumphee stared at the easterners. He wasn't too worried about Arapahos. He still had his M-16.

The engineer studied the tattered remains of Dumphee's army uniform, saw the canvas on the ATV stamped with U.S. Army. "If'n you Army boys would do your job, none of this would of happened. These plains are still crawling with redskin varmints. They ought to be exterminated. Injun troubles, Injun troubles—that's all we got!"

He looked at the ATV again and glanced around curiously. "What ya doin' with them elephant tusks?"

Dumphee couldn't think of any convincing lie, so he just said, "I'm going to carve them into piano keys and little figurines. It's a hobby of mine."

"When I was a kid, I always wanted to run off and join the circus," the engineer said. "Them are big tusks. You get them tusks from a circus?"

"No," Dumphee said, "I ordered them through the mail."

The engineer nodded suspiciously. "Where's your horses?"

Dumphee had no idea where he was, and he had the odd feeling that this fellow was going to start getting real personal real quick. He knew he wouldn't be able to answer the man's questions straight, so he decided to dazzle him with bull. "A Wookie ate 'em," Dumphee said. 'Bout forty miles north of here."

"Wookie?" the engineer asked. "Wookie?"

"Like a skunk ape, only taller. They'll rip a man's arms off, just for fun."

Now the engineer studied him with real wariness in his eyes. "What kind of soldier are you, anyway? Some kind of scout or somethin'?"

"Cyborg gunner," Dumphee said.

The engineer scrunched his forehead as if Dumphee had just spoken to him in Hindi.

"It's all top-secret stuff," Dumphee added. "I came out here looking for the plans to the Death Star. I ain't exactly sure where I am, but if'n you see Darth Vader, tell that shiftless varmint I'm gunnin' for him."

The engineer scratched his balding scalp in consternation. "Mister, you been kicked in the head by a mule or somethin'?"

Dumphee smiled and said in a placating tone, "I got some supplies here for the Army, but I need to get a message to, uh, my superiors. Do these telephone wires work?"

"Tele*graph*, you mean."

"Telegraph."

The engineer nodded. "I suppose the brakeman could shinny up one of them poles for you. Anything to get rid of these filthy warhoops."

CHAPTER 33

As Dumphee spoke with the engineer, Lotsa Smoke and the other squaws went to see the easterners. A bunch of them had wandered over to the half-burned station and were peering in the windows, pointing at the bloodstained floor where the stationmaster had been scalped.

It was a quiet, eerie place.

Lotsa Smoke peeked over a woman's shoulder. The woman's husband glanced back. "Look, Matilda," he said in a heavy English accent, "there's one of those filthy savages now!"

Lotsa Smoke tried to imitate his precise tone and mannerisms. "And I'm so pleased to make your acquaintance, too!" she replied.

The woman held up some spectacles on a stick, stared at Lotsa Smoke's beads and feathers. "Are those genuine Indian beads?"

Lotsa Smoke fingered the beads. Cheap Mayan things made of shells and wood. "Yeah. Wampum. You like?"

"Oh, Charles, you must buy them for me. The Everleys will be so jealous."

"What would you like for them?" the gentleman said. "A penny? Five cents?"

"One piece gold," Lotsa Smoke said. She was rich now, and didn't need to haggle with some man who had called her a "filthy savage." It wasn't as if she were a Seneca.

The fellow raised his eyes in shock, but his wife said quickly, "Oh, Charles, we must have them. This is a once-in-a-lifetime opportunity. In another five years, the Indians will all be wiped out. These beads are collectors' items."

"Well, all right," Charles said. He began digging into his money pouch.

But Lotsa Smoke frowned. In five years, her people would all be wiped out? She almost couldn't believe it.

Dumphee had promised that the Mohawks would survive. It was only the bad Indians who went extinct. But something in the woman's tone told Lotsa Smoke that Dumphee had lied. She recalled how Dumphee had choked on his answer. She began to seethe. She was staring into the faces of the men and women who would kill her people.

The man held out a gold coin.

Lotsa Smoke gave him a sour look. "Five piece, gold."

"Now look here!" the gentleman whined. "You told me one."

Lotsa Smoke raised a brow. "In five years, we Injun all be dead. Then where you buy wampum, huh? Five piece, gold."

"Oh, all right," he said, turning red in the face. "But I won't be taken advantage of."

Lotsa Smoke said with barely contained rage, "Me think you not the one be taken advantage of." She watched where he put his little wallet.

She made her sale, went back to the other squaws and talked conspiratorially. In moments, Bear Tail was out selling Mayan beads, calling out, "Wampum, wampum for sale."

Everywhere, the easterners gladly began gathering around. One man shouted, "Hey, Montgomery, come see this. Real Indian beads, by Jove." He held up the beads. "Look at that craftsmanship. It's hard to imagine that the savages could do such work!"

Bear Tail began to sell them cheap. The white men were using a new kind of money, called a "silver dollar," and the squaws had little idea how much such coins might be worth. They sold the beads at a dollar a string.

But Lotsa Smoke wrapped a blanket around her and walked through the crowd. After each sale, she would manage to bump an easterner, snatching wallets and purses, then dropping them into a basket hidden under her blanket.

She didn't need the money. She promised herself that she wouldn't even keep it. It was simply her way of striking back.

Meanwhile, Pretty Rose climbed into the train and began walking through the cars, looking into bags. She pulled coins and watches from purses, sometimes tossed a whole bag out the window, where it lay hidden at the bottom of the tracks.

CHAPTER 34

The brakeman carried a Leyden jar battery on a backpack, and had a telegraph key and his climbing spikes. He climbed up the telegraph pole to the wire, and the engineer asked Dumphee in his deep southern accent, "Now, y'all are sure there won't be no problem with the Army payin' for this call?"

"No problem at all," Dumphee said.

The brakeman got to the top of the pole and began tapping on the wire. In moments he called down. "It's workin'. Who do you want to send a message to?"

Dumphee stood a moment, dumbfounded. "Uh, what year is this?" he finally asked the engineer in embarrassment.

Very slowly, as if he weren't sure that Dumphee was sane, the engineer answered, "This is 1870, son."

"Sorry," Dumphee said. "I got shot in the head in the war. Sometimes my thoughts get kind of tangled.

"Well, if it's 1870, I guess I'd like to talk to, uh, General Sherman," Dumphee said, naming the first Northern Civil War general who came to mind.

The look the engineer gave Dumphee would have scared the fleas off a cat. The man's eyes blazed with tears and he shook with rage. "You want a couple of Georgia boys to place a call to Sherman for ya?" His tone became low and dangerous. "Old son, I don't think so!"

Dumphee suddenly realized that he'd left his weapons in the ATV. "Uh, did you think I said Sherman? Sherman the gol-danged arsonist? No, *suh!* I said *Sherwin*. General Sherwin. Sherwin Williams," he tried to speak the name with conviction, until he remembered that it was the name of a chain store that sold paint.

"Lyin' Yankee son of a mud-wallowin' buffalo," the engineer groused. "Get on out of here. An' I hope that feller blows the rest of your damned lousy brains out afore I do!"

Dumphee found his heart thumping. He called, "Ladies, ladies! I think it's time to go!"

CHAPTER 35

Just then, an English investor and his wife asked Lotsa Smoke, "No more wampum, you say? What about a toma-hawk, or some arrows or buckskins . . . any souvenirs. Maybe your blanket?"

Lotsa Smoke was backed into a corner, with nothing left that she wanted to sell. But then a crafty idea struck her. "I no have more wampum," she said. She reached into the bottom of her bag under her blanket. "But I have plenty scalps."

She pulled out the powdered wigs she'd taken from the Frenchman's quarters and thrust them into the English-man's face.

"Aaaaaaaah!" the wife screamed, then dropped in a faint. Everywhere, people began to shout and back away.

"Oh, oh, I say . . . I say," the Englishman blathered, shaking badly. "Those scalps weren't . . . uh . . . taken . . . here, were they?"

"Yes," Lotsa Smoke said calmly. "For you, only fifty dollar."

"Aaaaaagh!" he screamed.

A savvy miner lunged forward, grabbed the scalps and shook them in the air, shouting, "Men! Men! These are the varmints what burned the station!"

Behind her, someone shouted in wordless rage, lunged for her and made a grab. Lotsa Smoke threw off her blanket and wheeled away.

Beneath the blanket she was dressed in a breechcloth and breast-band, with a .45 holster tied to her right bare leg. She drew the automatic pistol and waved it at the easterners, who stared at it stupidly, as if unsure it was a real gun.

Bear Tail pulled out a wicked commando knife and a grenade, and leapt in beside Lotsa Smoke. The men raised their arms and backed off a step.

Up atop the telegraph pole the brakeman screamed in terror, and began waving frantically to the west, "Hostiles! Hostiles!"

A bullet fired from long distance hit a lantern of the station, sending it swinging. Another hit a fat lady in the bustle and made her jump.

For one moment, everyone stopped to look off to the west. A cloud of dust showed plainly where a hundred Indian warriors were riding hard.

Lotsa Smoke roared at the easterners, "Hah! Maybe in five minutes you all be wiped out!"

"Allll abooooard!" the engineer shouted as the brakeman slid down the telegraph pole. The fellow hit the ground hard and got up.

Dumphee stopped to pat the dust off and asked, "Are you all right?"

The brakeman scampered for the train, shouting, "Arapahos! Arapahos are comin'!"

Dumphee looked up at the engineer, who now was glaring at Dumphee in a fit of rage. "Filthy waaarhoooops," the engineer muttered, reaching into his waistband to pull out a long-barreled pistol.

Dumphee saw the gun, and dove for cover behind the telegraph pole just as the engineer opened fire. Bullets spattered all around him as he lay pinned to the ground. When the engineer had emptied his gun, he took one long glance behind him, then shouted again, "All aboard, goddamn it! Alll abooooard!" He began pulling levers and pushing pedals.

Up atop the train, a couple of men started shooting back at the Arapahos.

The train began pulling out without waiting for passengers, and in seconds the easterners were all running for their train.

"Let's go!" Lotsa Smoke shouted, dashing for the ATV.

Dumphee turned and raced for it, too. The braves began shouting war cries. A bullet pinged at Lotsa Smoke's feet.

Lotsa Smoke whipped past Dumphee, and jumped into the driver's seat of the ATV.

Dumphee leapt in beside her. Bear Tail behind. Pretty Rose shoved her way out of the train and dove into the back.

Lotsa Smoke slued around, and Bear Tail began digging through the back, looking for a weapon. Everything she grabbed was the experimental stuff. The easterners pulled out of the station while Lotsa Smoke punched the gas.

The ATV roared into high gear and slammed over the railroad tracks, almost leaping into the air. When it landed, Bear Tail and Pretty Rose fell into a heap.

"Stop!" Pretty Rose shouted. "Stop here!"

The ATV slammed to a halt. Pretty Rose leapt out, followed by the other squaws, and they began picking up the bags she'd thrown from the train.

Dumphee sat in his seat, astonished.

Lotsa Smoke opened one bag, pulled out a corset, studied it for a moment and threw it on her head with a whoop.

Bear Tail tried stuffing several smaller purses into one large trunk, but stopped to stare at a pair of red long underwear.

Pretty Rose had grabbed a tomahawk and now she used it to bash open the express box from the train. When it was opened, she whooped and threw gold coins in the air.

Dumphee looked off toward the cloud of dust. The warriors were still a good ways off, but riding fast. One of them leveled a rifle, fired. The bullet caromed off the ground.

Dumphee stared at the squaws, astonished. "You *robbed* those folks!" he said sadly. "You robbed them! What did you do it for?"

"What for?" Pretty Rose asked in surprise as she dragged the express box to the truck and heaved it in. "We got as much gold as from Mayan!"

"Yeah," Dumphee said as Bear Tail and Lotsa Smoke grabbed the last of the bags and heaved them into the back of the ATV, "but that's stealing. It's wrong."

Lotsa Smoke had pulled open a hatbox, and now she thudded a gorgeous ostrich-feather hat onto her head as if it were a helmet.

"Stealing?" she said, her voice pure acid. "What paleface do when he take whole country from Indian?" Her voice suddenly softened, became more solemn. "No, we learn good in missionary school. We very honest."

She giggled, no longer able to contain her amusement.

Dumphee shook his head in wonder. "You've got to mend your ways."

Lotsa Smoke started the truck, hit the gas. "Hmmm . . . good. Good," she said. "We mend ways. . . ." She got a dreamy faraway look in her eyes. "But first . . . we buy Chiefy hunting grounds like Sir William Johnson. Two—three valley, filled with deer and buffalo. Maybe couple rivers . . ." She thought for a moment, and added with a practical touch, "And maybe a dozen slaves to do squaw's work."

A bullet shattered the rearview mirror.

"Damn," Lotsa Smoke said. In the mirror's fragments, Dumphee could see Arapahos riding hard, still a couple hundred yards off.

Lotsa Smoke gunned the engine and began racing away. In the back, Pretty Rose and Bear Tail were still pulling stolen clothes out of boxes, inspecting children's clothes and watches. The sudden jerk of the ATV sent them toppling. Not far behind, the Arapahos began to whoop in delight.

Dumphee stared back. These were fierce-looking men in feathered war bonnets and buckskins. Their faces were painted, as were their rawhide shields and lances. Their rifles were decorated with eagle feathers.

The Arapahos leered at him, and Dumphee shouted, "I think we all best start shooting back!" just as another round went whizzing into the canvas of the ATV.

The braves near the front grabbed their reins in their teeth and a couple began nocking arrows.

"Good Lord," Dumphee said, "I think I'm in a John Wayne movie!"

Bear Tail looked around desperately for her M-16, but the back of the ATV was a disaster.

Lotsa Smoke swerved toward the train station, as if hoping to put the buildings between her and the warriors. As she did, she drove toward the water tower. Her right front bumper clipped one of the supports for the water tower, knocking it down.

Water splashed over the top of the ATV, ripped through the canvas and filled the back of it. Suddenly Pretty Rose and Bear Tail were swimming in the bed of the ATV. Everything was jumbled—gold, clothes, blankets. Bear Tail was busily trying to fill a buckskin bag with gold pieces.

Suddenly an Arapaho warrior nearby fired his rifle. The bag of gold busted.

Bear Tail snarled, "All right, you varmints! I fix you!"

A box of experimental weapons had floated up nearby. Pretty Rose took her tomahawk and smashed it open. It held a box of black tubes, like flares. Someone had stuck labels on the tubes, in English. Bear Tail held one up. It read *SAVAGE HARASSMENT, LEVEL 3 DETERRENT.*

"Ha, these weapon big! Powerful!" Pretty Rose shouted.

Pretty Rose hoisted it to her shoulder, while Bear Tail sighted down its barrel on the Arapaho warriors. Bear Tail shouted, "We blow Mingo to Hallelujah!" She pulled a lever.

Immediately the weapon emitted a sickening thunk and a flash of light.

Suddenly, all around the hooves of the Arapahos' horses, tiny Pekingese dogs appeared. They yapped and barked, ghost-like in the full light of day.

The mounts bucked wildly, and the warriors atop them snarled and let their arrows fly at the ghost dogs.

The tiny dogs turned and began barking *ki-yi-yi* as they fled in terror, following the truck.

The Arapahos raced forward, ignoring the dogs.

"Never min'," Pretty Rose said. "We got plenty more weapon! Try this!"

She reached into the box, pulled out a second tube. The label on it read *LEVEL 2 DETERRENT.*

"Hey," Dumphee shouted, "don't kill anybody!"

The squaws shouldered the weapon, pulled the trigger. Suddenly a dozen old grandmotherly women appeared, all with their gray hair tinted blue and put up in schoolmarm buns, all wearing flower-print dresses down past their knees and floating in the air. The ground seemed to move under their feet, even though they remained stationary. The air suddenly smelled of warm chocolate-chip cookies and milk.

The ghostly old women faced the warriors and shook their fingers. "Now, now," they said in unison. "Do you realize that your mother wouldn't approve of what you're doing!"

An Arapaho warrior screamed a fierce cry, slashed through a ghostly grandmother with a tomahawk, and all of the old women disappeared at once.

The warriors were drawing close now. One leapt from a painted pony and grabbed onto the rear of the ATV. Pretty Rose tried to push him off, but he grabbed her hand and held on, halfway dragging her from the ATV. Another Arapaho shot an arrow, puncturing the right rear tire.

Bear Tail screamed and grabbed a huge mortar from the pile. It was equipped with laser targeting sights and banks of green LED displays. The tag on it read *EXTREME EMERGENCY.*

Lotsa Smoke glanced back and shouted, "Son of bitch! Where gun?"

Dumphee looked back into the mess in the rear of the ATV, but couldn't see the M-16 beneath all of the flotsam. The warrior at the rear of the truck had half pulled Pretty Rose from the truck, only her feet were in. He had her by the hair and she was kicking and struggling as she bit into his ear.

Dumphee dove through the curtain into the back of the vehicle, fished through the slop for a weapon, but kept bringing up handfuls of gold coins instead.

Bear Tail growled, "This fix 'em," and aimed the huge mortar back, and let go.

The mortar shell landed with a thud amid the dirt, fifty yards behind the truck. Great black blobs floated up in the air, spinning ominously and hovering overhead.

Suddenly a barbershop quartet started up, men with Russian accents singing to the tune of "The Stars and Stripes Forever":

> Defect from the Red, White and Blue.
> Come to your friends in the trenches—

The ominous black blobs abruptly turned into huge turkeys on platters, dripping stuffing. The charging warriors all rode beneath them, staring up in wonder, and then actually slowed.

> You can make nice money too,
> And rendezvous with Russian wenches.

In the blur of a moment, the turkeys became dollar bills and scantily clad women so gorgeous that they made Heffner's Playboy Bunnies look positively tedious.

The whole war party brought their horses to a screaming halt and gazed upward expectantly as the Russian wenches lightly touched down. A couple of young Arapahos leapt from their mounts, hoping to wrestle the apparitions.

With all of the weight in the back of the ATV and a rear tire punctured, the ATV slowed and tipped, then began bouncing along over the rugged prairie.

Dumphee went to help Pretty Rose who still struggled with her attacker. He grabbed the warrior by his long hair, and yanked.

The fellow glared at him and cursed, pushed Pretty Rose aside and grabbed Dumphee's shirt collar. Dumphee tried to push the Arapaho back. He was sweaty and powerful. He held on to Dumphee and managed to swing onto the bumper of the ATV.

The young Arapaho glanced back at the warriors on their ponies, shouted for help. At just that moment, the Russian wenches touched ground and dissipated.

The war chief shook his rifle angrily, as if now doubly incensed, and urged the warriors to fan out and attack the wounded ATV. The Arapahos all spurred their mounts faster.

The chief himself fired at Dumphee, hit the left rear tire, so that it blew with a loud pop.

The truck began thudding over the prairie, jarring madly. The Arapahos raced around it. One rode up to the canvas, war lance raised threateningly. He hurled his lance at Bear Tail. It slashed through the canvas, narrowly missed her and came to rest on the floor of the ATV.

The truck jounced, throwing Bear Tail and Dumphee to the floor. The warrior who had Dumphee's collar twisted roughly and started to climb into the back of the ATV.

Dumphee grabbed the war lance and drove the butt of it into the warrior's belly, knocking him out of the truck.

Pretty Rose had been fishing in the bottom of the truck. She came up with a grenade, pulled the pin, counted to three and dropped it over the back of the ATV.

Three Arapahos racing up behind were thrown from their horses as the grenade exploded.

From the cab, Lotsa Smoke began screaming.

Dumphee craned his head around. There were horses with gunmen atop them riding up on each side of the ATV. Lotsa Smoke veered to the left, trying to drive one Arapaho brave away, then slued right, trying to hit the other. Gunfire crackled as the braves retaliated.

The truck raced up a steep slope, nosed high into the air, and for a moment went nearly vertical. Dumphee screamed and held on as everything in the truck shifted.

The ATV landed with a crash, enveloped in brightly colored mist. . . .

CHAPTER 36

Lotsa Smoke tried to slam the brakes on the ATV. It rolled madly ahead, clipped a telephone pole beside a blacktop road, slued sideways and hit a second telephone pole.

Dumphee shouted, "Stop!" and stared through the back of the truck.

"No can stop 'em truck, Chiefy!" Lotsa Smoke said, slamming the brake with all her might.

But Dumphee hardly noticed, his eyes fixed on the scene ahead. The truck roared past some Quonset huts along a blacktop road.

Straight ahead was a low block building painted in army green. A sign on it read *Experimental Weapons Battalion, Denver.*

"Grab the emergency brake!" Dumphee said as the truck neared the headquarters.

"Emergency brake? What that?" Lotsa Smoke shouted, trying to steer her way through a parking lot, past a master sergeant who dove for cover.

Dumphee sloshed forward, lunged over the seat and fumbled for the emergency brake and pulled hard.

The ATV rolled to a stop, the right front tire high on the steps of the command post. The engine belched steam, while water and women's underwear began pouring from the back of the truck onto the ground.

With a sick feeling, Dumphee opened the truck door and fell out on the ground, wondering what to do.

There was only one thing to do. He had to report to Major Slice.

His dress uniform was stained from months of wear, its gold buttons replaced with mismatched buttons made from ivory and copper. He'd lost his hat somewhere back in the Mesozoic, and the moccasins he wore were handmade by Mayans. He had a Russian commando knife slung on his hip, and he was still gasping and sweating after his struggle with some Indian brave.

With a sinking feeling, he realized that the worst part of this journey wasn't over.

Some civilian secretary came out of the headquarters and looked at the truck, at the squaws inside, and at Dumphee sprawled on the ground beside it. She screamed, "Major Slice! Major Slice!"

Dumphee decided he'd better go speak to the major quickly. Dumphee jumped up, dusted himself off, and hit the door just as the major came out of his office.

Dumphee shouted, "Private Dumphee reporting, sir!"

Slice gaped at him a long moment, mouth open. Obviously, he didn't recognize Dumphee at all. Dumphee didn't know what year it was, and wondered if he'd overshot his destination by a few years.

"Dumphee?" Slice asked. "You forgot to salute."

"Oh," Dumphee said, saluting once with each hand, not sure which to use.

Slice hardly seemed to notice. Instead he squinted suspiciously. "Where you been all this time, son?"

"Uh . . . it's kind of hard to say, sir. It was a very strange trip."

"Where's your cargo?"

"Right here, sir!" Dumphee said, saluting twice again for good measure.

As Dumphee fumbled with the door latch, Slice picked up the telephone, punched 0 for the base operator and whispered, "Get the MPs here, now!"

Dumphee yanked the door open to show the major the ATV. The squaws were still bouncing around in the truck, and just as Dumphee opened the door, the front right tire exploded in a hiss of air. The truck jounced once, its chassis clanging loudly against the concrete steps of the administration building, and disappeared in a haze of rose-colored fog. A loud bang like a thunderclap issued as air suddenly rushed in to occupy the void where the truck had once been.

Slice came to Dumphee's back. "So where is it?"

"It . . . it . . . was right there!" Dumphee said emphatically.

Slice stared at the water stains and the petticoats lying in the parking lot.

"You *lost* your cargo?" Slice asked.

"I swear, it was right there!"

A siren wailed as an MP jeep suddenly skidded to a halt in front of the administration building. Two MPs leapt from the jeep, brandishing automatic weapons.

"You poor, dumb son of a bitch," Slice said raising his hand and counting off on his fingers. "AWOL, desertion, out of uniform, insubordination, theft of government property!" When he was done counting off on his fingers, he raised the clenched fist. "You're going to grow old and die in the brig for this!"

CHAPTER 37

Once Dumphee was safely put away, with trembling hands Slice opened his address book and punched in a number. He didn't know exactly whom he was calling, but recognized the number as a prefix used only at the Pentagon.

The phone did not even ring before it was picked up. The speaker did not give his name or rank. Instead, he merely whispered, "Hello?"

Slice imagined that the room the fellow was in was dark and smoke-filled. It wasn't that fellow Smith or Jones or whomever he had spoken to before. "Uh, hello," Slice said, "This is—"

"We know who you are," the voice whispered. "Dumphee is there?"

"Yeah," Slice whispered back. "I didn't get too close. I didn't want to catch any temporal parasites or none of that crap."

"Smart fellow. He is under wraps?"

"Yeah," Slice said. "He's in quarantine over in one of the chemical weapons' decontamination units. No bail, no lawyers, and nobody to talk to."

"Good," the whispery voice said. "Colonel Kane will be with you shortly. ETA is . . . forty-seven minutes."

Slice glanced at his watch. A commercial flight from Washington, D.C., normally took five hours. Slice wondered if this Kane fellow was coming in a military jet, or if he was stashed away someplace closer, like Denver.

Exactly forty-four minutes later two men came into the front door of the headquarters—big blond-haired brutes in sunglasses and suits who looked so much alike that they could have been twins. Each of them stood nearly seven feet tall.

They surveyed the room ominously. The office door was open, and Slice's secretary peered at the guards, let out a little *eek* sound, then dashed from the room. No one needed to warn her to get out.

Slice knew that the government was riddled with secret organizations. Some of them, like M5, were open secrets that everyone knew about. But some of them were so secret that even their very names carried a Level 6 security classification. To speak the name of such an organization, even in one's sleep, might earn the death penalty.

Slice took one look at the goons and knew he was in trouble. He watched as they pulled out some hand-held devices that looked suspiciously like Tricorders from *Star Trek,* and scanned the room.

When they were satisfied, one spoke into a lapel mike, and in came Colonel Kane, wearing the same dark glasses.

Slice knew him by the names Smith, Jones. Whether his name was really Kane or not didn't matter. That was his name today.

Kane smiled dangerously.

"So, you have our man?"

Slice swallowed hard. "I'll take you to him." He got up, feeling weak in the knees, and raced from his office. Kane and his flat-faced guards followed at his heels. It wasn't until he reached his own sedan that he realized that he'd forgotten his swagger stick.

—ᴛᴛᴛ|ᴛᴛᴛ—

At Decontamination Chamber Four, Slice stood with Kane and his watchdogs at his back, and fumbled nervously with the huge key. A green light above the contamination chamber indicated that no one had opened the chamber door in the past hour.

Slice got the tumblers to click, then pulled open the heavy door slowly. It was as thick as the door of any bank vault, and just as heavy.

When the door swung outward, Slice stared in astonishment at the empty room with its padded walls.

"Escaped," one of the goons said.

"He . . . he . . . couldn't have!" Slice said in astonishment.

The burly guard pulled out his sensor device, pointed it at the room and waved it about. "I'm picking up a distinct temporal wake," he said ominously. "Someone discharged a time machine here within the past hour."

"Damn," Colonel Kane said grimly.

He walked to the center of the room, knelt down, and picked up a long, curved item from the floor.

"What's that?" Major Slice asked.

Kane held it up. It was a huge tooth, serrated along the inner edge, and covered in yellow tartar. "Tyrannosaur tooth," Kane replied. "A fresh one."

"I'll be damned," Major Slice said in awe.

Kane said, "Looks like he escaped with outside help."

"But . . . he couldn't have," Slice said. "This building is secure! No one could have gotten in or out!"

"Sure they could," Kane said. "A good operator could come, stand exactly on this spot a hundred years ago, or a million, and set the time machine to our day, so that they could pick Dumphee up, then go back, or forward. Did Dumphee mention the names of anyone who could have controlled the machines?"

"When we locked him up," Slice said, "he was raving about some squaws he picked up. But that was sophisticated equipment. Surely *they* couldn't learn to operate the thing!"

"Is that so improbable?" Colonel Kane asked. "After all, they had all the time in the world."

"Well . . ." Slice replied, unsure what to ask or say. "Can we catch the bastards?"

"We don't have that kind of manpower," Kane said. "We have no idea *when* to look."

"But . . . what now?"

Kane shook his head. "Case closed. As far as I can tell, Dumphee never showed up in any of the history books and never caused any disturbance. That's all we ask of him."

"But . . . isn't there anything more we can do?"

"We have bigger fish to fry," Kane said. "There's that whole Merlin and Camelot fiasco. . . ."

Kane pocketed the dinosaur tooth, turned as if to leave, then stared hard at Major Slice. "You'll be coming with us. Reassigned."

"Coming with you?" Slice said. He knew by Kane's tone that he had no other option. He could go with Kane, or he could die. "When—I mean, I'll have to tell my wife, make arrangements to move."

"You have no wife," Kane said. "You have nothing to move. You know too much, and so you'll simply disappear, and become one of us. You have no choice."

"But, who are we?" Slice begged.

"Time Police," one of the goons said.

"I'll be damned!" Slice said in astonishment.

Kane smiled grimly, "Yes, sir. You certainly are."

CHAPTER 38

Dumphee sat uncomfortably in his tuxedo and white bow tie and gazed out the window of an exclusive Parisian restaurant at the Eiffel Tower. A chamber orchestra was playing in the background of the private dining room, but Dumphee hardly paid attention.

Lotsa Smoke sat at his right, wearing a splendid white evening gown with a beaded buckskin jacket thrown over it. To his left, Bear Tail wore a dusky blue dress with a diamond tiara. A single eagle feather was tucked stylishly in back, and a cigar was clenched between her teeth. Across the table, Pretty Rose stared at Dumphee in the candlelight, her eyes shining. While she waited for the appetizer, she absently cleaned under her fingernails with a commando knife.

The manager of the establishment set a silver champagne chiller filled with ice on the table, drew out the dust-covered bottle, then bent low beside Dumphee's ear and whispered urgently, "*Monsieur,* nothing but our very finest for you!"

He held the bottle to display a forty-two-year-old label. Dumphee stared at the man's face, surprised. The manager looked astonishingly like the brothers at *Pierre et Pierre*— probably a distant grandson.

"No," Lotsa Smoke growled. "Firewater no good for Chiefy." She grabbed the bottle and banged it against the table, breaking off the top. Foam spilled out. Then she poured the champagne into the chiller with a slosh and hurled the bottle back over her head. It shattered on the floor, and the manager hurried to clean it up with a towel.

"A *little* firewater never hurt a West Virginia boy," Dumphee said, but Lotsa Smoke pushed the bucket away, eyeing him cagily.

"No," she argued, "must keep head clear for tomorrow, sell jaguar god. Man only offer ten million dollar."

Lotsa Smoke picked up the bucket herself, took a long draft of champagne, and then hurled the bucket over her head. She smiled at him sweetly and said, "Oh, how nice to be civilize!"

Dumphee stared at her in astonishment, just as she reached in to adjust his white bow tie.

About the Authors

L. RON HUBBARD

Born in a rugged and adventurous Montana, L. Ron Hubbard lived a life of truly legendary proportions. Before the age of ten, he had already broken his first bronco and earned that rare status of blood brother to the Blackfeet Indians. By age eighteen, he had logged more than a quarter of a million miles, twice crossing the Pacific—before the advent of commercial aviation—to a then still mysterious Asia. Returning to the United States in 1928, he entered The George Washington University where, drawing from far-flung experience, he began to shape some of this century's most enduring tales.

By the mid-1930s the name L. Ron Hubbard had graced the pages of some two hundred classic publications of the day, including *Argosy, Top-Notch* and *Thrilling Adventures*. Among his more than fifteen million words of pre–1950 fiction were tales spanning all primary genres: action, suspense, mystery, westerns, and even the occasional romance. Enlisted to "humanize" a machine-dominated science fiction, the name

L. Ron Hubbard next became synonymous with such utterly classics as *Final Blackout* and *To the Stars*—rightfully described as among the most defining works in the whole of the genre. No less memorable were his fantasies of the era, including the perennially applauded *Fear,* described as a pillar of all modern horror.

After the founding of DIANETICS® and SCIENTOLOGY® (the fruition of research actually financed through those fifteen million words of fiction), Ron returned to the world of popular fiction with two monumental blockbusters: the internationally bestselling *Battlefield Earth* and the ten-volume MISSION EARTH® series—each volume likewise topping international bestseller lists in what amounted to an unprecedented publishing event. His screenplays, now being turned into novels, continued this tradition, when in 1998, *Ai! Pedrito!—When Intelligence Goes Wrong* (novelized by Kevin J. Anderson) became his fourteenth fiction *New York Times* bestseller.

In 1983, and in what has been described as the culmination of a lifetime commitment to fellow authors, L. Ron Hubbard directed the founding of the *Writers of the Future* Contest. Dedicated to the discovery and encouragement of new talent within the realms of speculative fiction, the Contest has since proven both an integral part of the greater L. Ron Hubbard literary legacy and the most successful competition of its kind. Accordingly, Contest judges have comprised the most celebrated names of the genre, including Frederik Pohl, Orson Scott Card and Frank Herbert. To date, the Contest has helped place some 250 novels from new authors on worldwide bookshelves.

DAVE WOLVERTON

Following that April 1987 evening at the World Trade Center in New York, when it was announced that Dave Wolverton was the winner of the L. Ron Hubbard Gold Award for the *Writers of the Future* Story of the Year—and a check for $4,000—Dave's career has been on a steady rocket ride.

His winning short story published in *L. Ron Hubbard Presents Writers of the Future,* Volume III, "On My Way to Paradise," was the basis for his first novel (same title), which won the Philip K. Dick Memorial Special Award as one of the outstanding science fiction novels of the year in 1989.

His "Star Wars" novel, *The Courtship of Princess Leia,* was a *New York Times* and *USA Today* bestseller and was among the Top 40 hardcover fiction bestsellers of 1994 in the *Publishers Weekly* end-of-the-year report.

Along with his eleven published novels, he has published dozens of short stories and one, "After a Lean Winter," was a recent finalist for the Nebula Award in the short-story category.

In addition to writing fiction, Dave Wolverton has his hand in shaping fiction, as the coordinating judge of the internationally acclaimed L. Ron Hubbard's *Writers of the Future* Contest, the world's largest contest for writers of science fiction, fantasy and horror. In his capacity as judge, he acts as first reader and teaches *Writers of the Future* writers workshops.

Not one to take it easy, Dave Wolverton works with Saffire Corporation, a Utah video-game producer, assisting in developing properties for the gaming industry. Some recent projects include design work on *StarCraft's Brood Wars*, the Xena fight game for Nintendo 64 and development of *The Young Olympians*—a series of books, comics and video games.

This year, aside from the novel *A Very Strange Trip*, there will also be another Dave Wolverton movie-script-based book, a juvenile "Star Wars," from *Episode I: The Phantom Menace.*